hearts *of* iron

Also by Kathleen Benner Duble

The Sacrifice

Margaret K. McElderry Books

hearts *of* iron

kathleen benner duble

Margaret K. McElderry Books
New York London Toronto Sydney

Margaret K. McElderry Books
An imprint of Simon & Schuster Children's Publishing Division
1230 Avenue of the Americas, New York, New York 10020

Book design by Michael McCartney
The text for this book is set in Caslon.

Manufactured in the United States of America
10 9 8 7 6 5 4 3 2 1

Library of Congress Cataloging-in-Publication Data
Duble, Kathleen Benner.
Hearts of iron / Kathleen Benner Duble.—1st ed.
p. cm.
Summary: In early 1800s Connecticut, fifteen-year-old Lucy tries to decide whether to marry her childhood friend who unhappily toils at the Mt. Riga iron furnace or the young man from Boston who has come to work in her father's store.
ISBN-13: 978-1-4169-0850-0
ISBN-10: 1-4169-0850-1 (hardcover)
[1. Conduct of life—Fiction. 2. Courtship—Fiction.
3. Metallurgical furnaces—Fiction. 4. Connecticut—
History—1775–1865—Fiction.] I. Title.
PZ7.D8496Hea 2006
[Fic]—dc22
2005029258

For Mara,

my joy-sharer,

my shoulder to cry on,

my most helpful critic

and biggest advocate,

my soulmate,

and oh yes,

I almost forgot—

my sister!

Acknowledgments

As I stand beside the remnants of the furnace on Mount Riga and listen to the wind with its stories blowing across the now empty meadow, I have to first acknowledge the people who tirelessly worked this town for forty-odd years. They were a hardy lot, and I hope I have done them justice in this book.

To my husband, Chris Duble, thank you for introducing this community to me.

To my daughters, Liza and Tobey, thanks for giving me those wonderful days on the mountain painting, reading, swimming, boating, and laughing—which I will never forget! (Remember the cannibal and the turtle!)

To the current "Raggies," thank you for the many lovely summer nights of good food, fine wine, and great conversation. I truly believe you still embody the spirit of those who came before you, cherishing the beauty and the solitude of the mountain.

To Donna McArdle and Marcia Strykowski, many thanks for helping me find the right mix of words and fire to create a blend of metals Sarah would find acceptable.

To JoAnn Reed, many thanks for proofing my galleys, adding your words of wisdom, and "proving" the final product.

And lastly, to Sarah Sevier, who has once more forged a manuscript into a truer and more perfect shape, I thank you for the lessons I learn from you every time we work together.

1.

Lucy Pettee stood on the edge of the cliff in nothing but her shift, and closed her eyes. A light breeze ruffled her hair, made the skin on her arms rise in goose bumps, sent a shiver down her back.

"I can't," she called out to Jesse.

"Baby!" Jesse taunted.

"It's too cold," Lucy yelled, still keeping her eyes tightly shut. If she looked down, even for a second, she knew she'd turn back. She hated heights.

"No, it ain't," Jesse shouted. "It's warm, Luce. It's really, really warm."

Lucy imagined Jesse's glee as he paddled around in the water and saw the fear on her face.

"Liar!" Lucy shouted out at him, finally opening her eyes.

Below her, Jesse was grinning.

"Trust me, Luce," Jesse shouted up. "It's hot, hot, hot."

Lucy looked at the impossible distance between where she stood and the water below. Her stomach lurched, and she wished for the hundredth time in one day that she was not so impossibly bigmouthed and quick to take a dare.

She shut her eyes again. "It's never hot in that water in May, and you know it, Jesse Rosseter."

"Don't do it then, Luce," Jesse yelled. "Forget about it."

Lucy's eyes shot open again. Was he kidding? Was he letting her off the hook?

Jesse drifted on his back. "Course that means I win. You done promised last summer you'd be in the water with me before anyone else, and from the cliff, too."

"That was last summer, Jesse," Lucy protested. She swayed a bit, and quickly shut her eyes again. "Besides, it was June when you first went in last year. Not May."

"Let's see," Jesse's lazy voice floated up from the water. "I believe you said that you could go in just as good as me, anytime and from anywhere. If you don't jump, Luce, I reckon that means you'll be putting a dead mouse in old Grandma Brazee's sewing kit. Weren't that the bet we made?"

Lucy's anger rose. "Yes, that was the bet, Jesse Rosseter. That sure was the bet!"

And, without thinking, a trait quite common to Lucy Pettee, she jumped. She had an odd sensation of nothing, then of her stomach coming up to join her throat. Down, down, down she went into the depths of the lake. The coldness stole her breath and most of her thoughts, except that she had been a fool. Lucy swam for the surface, fighting her wet shift, and finally broke the water, gasping for air.

From a distance, she could hear laughter. Jesse was already out, hopping around on the banks of the lake as he pulled on his pants and suspenders.

"You liar!" Lucy shouted out. "It's freezing!"

"Sure is," Jesse said, shaking his head. "Thought you'd never jump. Thought I'd be a goner with frostbite, you took so long."

"I'm going to kill you, Jesse," Lucy yelled.

Jesse let out a howl of laughter, and with hurried strokes, Lucy began swimming toward him.

Her heart was beating wildly from the fright of falling, and she could not remember a time when she had been so chilled. And how, she wondered, would she get her undergarment dry in this weather without catching her death of cold? She should have thought of all this earlier, she realized ruefully. Lucy pulled harder and harder toward the shore.

Finally her foot found rocks, and she stood up. As the wind touched her skin, she threw her arms around herself—though what good it would do, she had no idea.

Jesse was climbing back down from the cliff, where he had gone to retrieve her clothes.

"You did it, Luce," he said, smiling. "All those years you've been watching me make that jump, and you finally found the courage. You gotta be proud of that!"

"I'd be prouder if I wasn't freezing," Lucy said, although Jesse's words had warmed her some. "Look away, Jess. I've got to get out of this wet clothing."

Dutifully, Jesse turned. Lucy pulled down the straps of her shift and struggled to loosen the dripping cotton from her body. She hesitated for a minute, but there was really no way around it. She would have to take the undergarment off completely.

"Need a little help?" Jesse teased, moving just slightly.

"Don't you dare, Jesse," Lucy warned.

"Oh, come on, Luce, let me help you out there," Jesse joked. "After all, I did go get those clothes for you."

"And if it wasn't for you, I wouldn't be without my clothes in the first place," Lucy snapped. "Keep your head turned, Jess."

Jesse chuckled, but did as Lucy told him. Lucy knew he would. He always treated her respectfully, even if he gave her no leeway for being a girl. Still, lately sometimes things had seemed different. Lucy hurried to slip her dress back on, followed by her stockings and starched cap.

"All right. You can turn around," Lucy said as she finished the last of her buttons.

Jesse faced her and spat on his hand. "Good work, partner," he said. "Now that you've jumped from that cliff, we've done it all together."

Lucy spit on her own hand and rubbed it with Jesse's warmer one. She smiled at him.

Ever since she could remember, with the exception of the cliff, Lucy had followed Jesse Rosseter wherever he'd gone. They had met when they were four, when Lucy and her father had first come to the mountain in 1810. They'd liked each other the minute they'd seen each other, both dirty and bruised from playing too hard. She'd followed him into all kinds of trouble that day, and had continued to every day from then on. Whether they were standing too near the iron forges or blast furnace that ran on the lower lake, or skipping out on their chores by running high into the mountain to the upper lake, or pulling pranks on the navy admirals and captains who came from Washington once a year, it was always Jesse and Lucy—a team. They were best pals. Always would be.

Jesse bent and picked up a stone. He sent it skipping out over the lake, then scowled. "Only eight," he grumbled.

"I can do more," said Lucy, bending to pick up a stone too. She was still cold, and her hand shook as she held it. She let the stone fly. Eight skips.

"Same," Jesse said.

"I can do more," Lucy insisted. She bent and picked up another stone.

"You can't," Jesse said. "We ain't never gotten more than eight."

"Don't say 'never,' Jess," Lucy said. "I hate that word." She drew back her arm and fired. Five skips.

"See?" Jesse asked. "Eight's the best we're ever gonna get." He sat down on a rock.

"We can beat it. I know we can," Lucy said, but she gave up thinking of skipping stones and went and sat down next to Jesse. The lake and the land around it were just starting to show signs of new life. The mountain laurel was beginning to bloom, and the birds were returning from the south. From far off came the smell of burning wood. Lucy looked out at the stillness of the water and the mountains that rose beyond it. She loved this lake. She loved these mountains. She loved her life.

"Jesse Rosseter," came a stern voice.

Ezra Ostrander stood on the rocks above them. "Yer pa's been looking everywhere for ya, son. They're preparing the blast furnace to start up tomorrow, and he needs ya to be home and help out."

Jesse stared glumly back at the lake. He didn't answer Mr. Ostrander.

Lucy put her head near Jesse's. "That's the one place I can *never* follow you, Jess," she whispered softly.

"You wouldn't want to, Luce," Jesse mumbled back, his usually happy face now sour.

"And as for you, Lucy," Mr. Ostrander continued, "I ain't believing yer pa would be happy about ya being out here swimming and not about yer womanly chores at home."

Lucy scowled up at Mr. Ostrander. He was such a busybody. She wondered why he always seemed more interested in the way other children behaved than how his own did. Maybe it was because they were such a quiet, well-behaved, boring lot.

"And . . . ," Mr. Ostrander continued, but then his voice went strangely silent.

Lucy followed his gaze to her wet shift on the rock. Lucy could see the old man's mind working and the realization dawning in his eyes that she had somehow taken off her undergarment, even though she was now fully dressed. The evidence spoke for itself: At one point in the recent past, Lucy had stood here unclothed. Her heart sank.

"Lucy Pettee," Mr. Ostrander commanded, "I reckon ya best come with me right this here instant. And bring that . . . that . . . that clothing with ya."

Reluctantly, Lucy stood and picked up the soaked shift. Already she could imagine the soreness on the back of her legs, where she knew she'd feel her father's strap.

Jesse smiled slightly. "Think about the jump, Luce," he whispered. "Remember the jump. And you'll know it was worth it."

Lucy snorted. "Easy for you to say. You aren't the one taking the whipping."

Jesse gave a quiet chuckle as Lucy climbed the hill toward the waiting Mr. Ostrander and the knowledge that she was in trouble once again.

2.

Lucy sat out on the porch, shelling peas and trying to keep from sniffling. Her legs felt as if they were on fire, but she had not cried as she received her whipping, and she was proud of that.

On the mountain road below, Lucy could see wagons leaving the lower lake, making their way back down the mountain. The horses would be snorting in relief, having just this morning made the haul from town carrying loads of iron ore for the blast furnace's opening tomorrow.

Her father moved about in the kitchen, putting away the strap he had just used. He sighed. Lucy knew he hated whipping her, but with Mr. Ostrander bringing her home, he had been left little choice but to punish her.

Lucy heard him coming her way, and then the

sound of the screen door swinging open and banging shut. Her father moved across the porch, sat in his rocker, and began slowly rocking back and forth. He sighed again.

"Didn't like having to do that, Lucy," he finally said.

"I know," Lucy said. "I'm sorry."

Her father cleared his throat. "I understand that you don't like Mr. Ostrander, Luce," he went on, "but he's right. You *are* getting too old to go swimming in just your shift with Jesse."

He paused. "Or with any boy for that matter," he said in a soft tone.

Lucy was puzzled by this conversation. As long as she could remember, it had been just her and her father. They had come to the mountain a year after Lucy's mother died from consumption. The mountain had been her father's way to bury his pain from that loss. Still, after all these years alone, he was never comfortable with discussions on womanly topics.

Usually Lucy spared him any questions she could by asking Jesse's mother about the changes she'd felt, and Mrs. Rosseter had always spoken honestly to Lucy. So she wondered why her father was bringing this subject up now, when the whipping should have been enough said on the matter.

"Maybe you and Jess are getting too old to be in each other's company so much anymore, anyway," her father said lightly.

Lucy gasped. She turned toward her father with wide, frightened eyes.

"Now, now, child," he said, his cheeks flushed with embarrassment, "don't go getting crazy on me. I'm not saying you can't see him at all, maybe just not so much."

"Why not?" Lucy asked, her voice shaking, her mind wild at the thought of not spending all her days with Jesse.

Her father looked down at the porch floor, shifting uncomfortably again on the rocker. "I know he's your friend, Lucy," he said, "and I know how much you care about each other. I don't mean you can't see him at all, but the boy's going to be busy working at the furnace now. His pa is expecting him to take on responsibility, like he should."

"He hates the furnace," Lucy said.

Her father sighed. "I know that, Luce. Anyone who knows Jesse knows that. But that's what's here for him to do. There's not much else on this mountain, other than a little farming, and that doesn't pay half as much. I'm afraid it's the life Jesse is going to have. He'll come around to it."

"No, he won't," Lucy said firmly.

"Lucy," her father said, "please don't speak to me like that. And there isn't any use in talking to Jesse like that either. Ironwork is what he's got to do, and it's what he will do." Her father shrugged. "Besides, the work isn't that bad."

"How would you know?" Lucy muttered. "You're a shopkeeper."

Her father sighed. "Must you make me get out the strap again tonight, Lucy?"

"No, sir," Lucy said quickly. Just the thought of another whipping made her legs ache again. "I'm sorry."

Her father leaned back. The creaking back and forth resumed, a little quicker, a little more forceful. "It's time you take your place as a woman, anyhow,

Lucy," he repeated. "It's what I want for you."

Lucy listened without enthusiasm. She had already taken her place as a woman, if you asked her. She did all the washing, the cleaning, the planting and weeding of the garden, the candle-making, the spinning, the cooking and canning. What more was there?

"I think it's time you started thinking on marriage, Lucy," her father said.

Lucy turned and stared at her father again. "Marriage?" she said. "But, Father, I'm not old enough."

Her father smiled. "Your mother was sixteen when we married, and you're almost fifteen. That's old enough to start thinking on it, anyway. I've been writing some folks back home, seeing who might be available to take on a wife."

"Back home?" Lucy whispered. "You want me to marry someone from Boston?"

"There isn't anyone here for you, Lucy," her father said. "I can't have you married to someone who works the furnace or forges. You come from better stock than that."

"But, Father," Lucy protested, "these are the

people we know, the people we live with. Are you saying that the folks on the mountain aren't good enough for me?"

"No, Lucy," her father said. "I'm saying they're not good enough for you to marry. I know they have money, what with being such skilled labor, but they have no manners and not much education. Besides, what kind of life is it on this mountain? I came here because I needed to leave behind the memories of your mother, but I won't have you stuck up here forever. I care about you too much to see that happen."

"I'm not stuck," Lucy cried out. "I love this mountain, Father."

"I know you do," her father said, rising from his rocker, "but you'll change your mind when you get to Boston. The city has a lot to offer, things this mountain can never provide, no matter how much money is here."

"I don't want to go to Boston," Lucy said. "I don't want to leave the mountain or Jesse or you. I can't."

Her father stopped at the door. "It'll be hard, Lucy, I know. I'll miss you, too. But it's best for you, and as your father, I've got to think on that. And if it's marriage with Jess you're considering, you can forget it right now. Jesse Rosseter is a good boy. I like him, but he's not the man for my daughter. His ways are too rough, child. Now finish your shelling."

Her father went back inside, and Lucy stared at the peas in front of her. Marry? Marry someone she had never met from Boston? Leave the mountain? Impossible. She would die if she had to do that.

But marriage with Jesse? That thought had never crossed her mind either. She loved Jesse. He was her best friend. And although she had never thought of him as anything but that, she had to admit that lately she *had* felt funny with him sometimes. But funny in a good way.

Could she marry Jesse? When she thought of it, she couldn't really imagine marrying anybody but Jesse. Still—marriage to anyone? Lucy couldn't believe her father was actually talking about it!

These were thoughts she didn't want, and she pushed them resolutely from her mind. She'd worry about it when the time came, when her father actually had someone reply to him. She could argue with him then.

And really, who would respond? She was a little nobody from a strange forging town on a lonely mountain in Connecticut. What *good* family would want her?

No, she thought, *no one will want a girl with no social graces and no real homemaking skills to brag about.*

And if they came to look her over, they'd find only a skinny little thing with too many freckles, skinned-up knees, and so much red hair that no comb could control it. They'd run away faster than the hares in the meadow when they heard a shotgun. She was sure of it.

That decided, she picked up the bowl of peas and returned to the shelling. If she didn't hurry, supper would be late. She hoped that her father's request for her to not see Jesse as much had been provoked by the swimming. She was sure it was just the embarrassment of having Mr. Ostrander bring her home that had prompted all this crazy talk. Maybe if she was really good the next few days, he would forget the whole idea. Then life could return to normal.

"Psst." Lucy looked up from her shelling. Jesse

was hiding behind some trees at the edge of the woods by her house.

"You all right?" he called softly, stepping out and coming closer.

Lucy nodded. "No thanks to you," she replied, laughing as she always did with him. Yet looking at Jesse now, standing there, she was acutely aware of the sunlight on his arms and the way his hair curled on the nape of his neck. She squirmed and bit her lip and cursed her father for making her see Jesse in this way.

"I expect I can't come sit with you on the porch?" he asked.

"You got that right," she said, wishing he could come and sit awhile so they could talk like the friends they were, until these strange feelings she was experiencing would float away on the spring breezes, back to where they had come from.

"Guess I'll be on my way home then," Jesse said. "See you tomorrow."

"All right," Lucy agreed.

Jesse disappeared back into the shadows of the woods. Lucy watched him go, her heart fluttering in her chest. But a minute later, he came again to the edge of the wood.

"Luce?" he called softly.

"Yes?"

"You know I would have taken that whipping for you if I could've," he said.

"I know that," Lucy said, smiling.

"Night, Luce," Jesse said.

"Good night, Jess," she called back.

"Lucy?" Her father's voice came from the house. "Somebody out there?"

"No, Father," Lucy replied. "It's just me." And it was. Jesse was gone.

"Well," her father said, "how's that supper coming?"

Sighing, Lucy stood and picked up the bowl of peas. In that moment she had a sudden image of doing the same thing for some man other than her father. The idea made her shudder.

No, she thought, steeling her mind against it. *It will not happen. I will not marry, not for a long, long time.*

Then she made her way inside to finish the supper.

3.

Lucy woke the next morning to the familiar sound of the blast furnace up and running. The noise was deafening, and Lucy could already picture the flames shooting from the furnace, and the men's faces as they drove the horses across the walkway to the top of the stone structure, their wagons loaded full of charcoal, lime, and ore. For the next five months, the furnace would run nonstop, its smoke darkening the skies, its flames providing raging light. Bellows would creak with the weight of the water in the wheels used to power them, and sigh their breaths into the flames. The forge buildings below would ring out the sound of hammers on metal, shaping everything from household items, such as tools, kettles, and nails, to anchors and chains for the United States Navy.

Lucy would miss the peacefulness of the winter months, when work was minimal and no one came from down off the mountain. The whole town, all forty-two homes, would wrap themselves around each other, visiting to quilt or gather firewood, meeting after supper in various homes to listen to one or another mountain man play his fiddle. She loved those months of mountain solitude.

Starting today, the furnace would spill forth its fumes until October. But it was why she and her father were here, why everyone was here. So as she did every time the furnace began again, she reminded herself it was the iron that let her have those winter months of joy and peace in the first place.

Lucy threw back the covers and swung her feet onto the cold wooden floorboards. Although spring was here, the mornings were still chilly. Hurriedly she threw a shawl over her nightdress. She would get the Franklin stove up and running, and then she would change for school.

Lucy brought some wood into the kitchen from where it was piled near the back porch. Then she leaned over and opened the door to the iron stove.

She crumpled up some paper, laid a few logs on top, and set a match to the pile. Soon the fire was blazing, and she closed the door to let the heat of the fire warm the top of the stove. She picked up an iron pot, crafted at the forge on the mountain, and filled it with water from the pump over the sink, her arm working the handle up and down until the pot was full. Then she set it on the stove to boil for coffee.

Her father came into the kitchen, already dressed.

"Last week of school, and you're up late," he said, giving her his best stern look.

Lucy knew he wasn't angry. Her father could rarely sustain being mad at her for more than an hour or so, and never overnight. "I'll hurry to get breakfast fixed," she assured him.

Her father shook his head. "Don't bother for me, Luce," he said. "I've got to go down off the mountain today, into town. I've got a shipment coming from France. Supposed to be some real fine silks in this one, and I'm going to see if I can sell some before I bring everything up the mountain."

"Don't let Grandma Brazee hear about that," Lucy

warned. Grandma Brazee was the oldest woman on the mountain, and everyone called her Grandma. For years, she had ruled the community with her sharp tongue and opinions. Because the mountain was so small, everyone eventually knew everyone else's business, but no one knew it quicker than Grandma Brazee.

Her father grinned. "I guess she'd finish me off if she thought I was selling to townies before mountain people. Still, it just makes sense to off-load a little down there rather than dragging it all up here. I know those townies will climb the mountain anyhow to get that French silk, but as long as I have to go down, I might as well make it a tiny bit easier for them."

Lucy scowled. "For once, I agree with Grandma Brazee," she said. "I don't see why we need to go out of our way for people who aren't mountain folk."

Her father shrugged. "It's not out of my way, and they're still customers, Luce."

Lucy was about to say more when it occurred to her that if her father went down off today, she might have breakfast at the Rosseters' before school. Her father would be none the wiser, and in the afternoon, she would be the obedient daughter and stay at home, doing her chores. If she did all of them and did them well, perhaps her father would be pleased, and his normal good mood and leniency would be restored.

Just the thought of having breakfast with Jesse and his large, noisy family rather than sitting here alone made her smile. A half hour with the Rosseters would return everything to normal. Besides, her father had suggested she not see Jesse *as much*, not never.

Her father grabbed his hat from a hook by the door. "Be back for supper," he said.

Lucy nodded.

He placed the hat on his head. "Might just have a little something for you too, Luce, when I get back."

"Really?" Lucy asked. "What?" Her father rarely brought her presents, though he could afford to.

But her father just smiled. "You'll have to wait and see," he said. He kissed her on the forehead and walked out the door.

Out in the yard, he hitched up the wagon for the four-mile trip down the mountain. He bent slightly, and for a quick moment, Lucy envisioned the old man her father would become. The thought caused her to pause a moment.

When they had first come to the mountain, the community needed a shopkeeper, one knowledgeable in high-end goods. Even though the ironworkers were a rough lot, they liked fine things, and the items in the mountain store showed it. The shop carried the best of everything. That was why even the people in the town at the foot of the mountain rode up to do some of their purchasing at her father's store.

Before Lucy's mother died, her father had owned a fancy shop on Newbury Street in Boston. He knew quality when he saw it, and he knew where to get it. Lucy's father had described the store to her. It had stood on a wide street surrounded by other shops. In the city, carriages lined the avenues and people walked about. To Lucy, it had sounded like a crowded and ugly place, without the grace, charm, and peacefulness of the mountain. She was glad her father had come here to heal his wounds. *But now,* she thought, *he might just send me back.* And what would he do? Stay here without her, growing old alone?

A log fell in the fire and startled Lucy from her thoughts. She had better get herself moving. She would have to hurry if she wanted to have breakfast with the Rosseters and still be on time for school.

She went to her room and put on a shift, dress, and starched cap. She threw a shawl around her shoulders and gathered up her books. Then she tossed an apple, a slice of buttered bread, and some smoked sausage into a basket and hurried out into the cold morning air.

Outside, the sounds of the furnace and forges were louder than ever. Lucy made her way from her house high on the hill down the rutted dirt road toward the lower lake and the Rosseters' house. When she rounded the bend, she could see flames shooting from the top of the stone furnace, and the hustle and bustle of the men working the iron. She couldn't make out anyone in particular but could see that they were all moving fast and furiously. It always started out with this kind of speed, when the men were fresh for working after a long white winter. But a few months into the running, the pace would slow. Accidents would happen. Everyone would be looking forward to the fall, when the blast furnace would lay quiet again and the job would be finished for the winter.

"That you, Lucy?" came an old, crackly voice.

On the porch of a large wooden house, Grandma Brazee leaned forward in her rocker. Lucy sighed. How could Grandma see Lucy on the road when she was constantly telling everyone that she couldn't handle the chores around her house because of her poor eyesight?

"I said," came the voice, more imperious now, "is that you, Lucy Pettee?"

"Yes, Grandma," Lucy responded. "It's me."

"Well, come sit a spell with me," Grandma said. "Being alone all day's a lonely thing for a blind old woman like me."

You aren't so blind you can't catch unsuspecting folk just trying to pass by, Lucy thought. Her stomach growled with hunger, and she would be late for school if Grandma talked too long. Still, she would have to stop, if only for a minute, or her father would hear about it. Grandma Brazee's requests were to be denied by no one.

Reluctantly, Lucy climbed the rickety old porch

steps to where Grandma Brazee sat on her rocker with a quilt over her lap. Gray hairs curled from her chin.

"Heard you had a bit of a whipping yesterday," Grandma Brazee said. She rocked back and forth.

Lucy scowled. There were absolutely *no* secrets on this mountain!

"Don't make faces at me, young lady," Grandma said. "Ain't no place for a girl your age to go swimming with just her shift on. And with a boy at that."

"It was just Jess, Grandma," Lucy said impatiently.

Grandma Brazee howled, throwing back her head. "Just Jesse," she said, gasping as if to catch her breath. "Oh, Lucy, if you don't know by now that that boy is sweet on you, your pa ain't raised you to take notice of nothing."

"Jess is just my friend, Grandma," Lucy protested.

Grandma nodded knowingly. Her supposedly blind eyes turned toward Lucy. "Friends is a fine way to begin. It's the way I began with Grandpa Brazee, God rest his soul."

Lucy shook her head. Why was everyone acting like she and Jesse were more than friends? They weren't, were they? Was it possible that Jesse thought of her as more, even though he had never said as much? Could everyone else have seen something she never had?

Suddenly the old woman shot forward, clutching her chest. "Lordy," she called, making Lucy jump.

Grandma fumbled with the front of her shirt. Reaching a hand inside, she drew out a baby chicken.

"Looks like I got a new one, eh, Lucy?" Grandma was rubbing the newly hatched chicken with her fingers. Inside her blouse, two more eggs were nestled next to the old woman's wrinkled chest.

"Like I tell everyone," Grandma Brazee crowed, "the best way to warm these little critters is next to your own heart, rather than in them drafty old barns around here. I got more chickens than anyone else on the mountain, ain't that so?"

The woman was crazy. "I have to be going now, Grandma, or I'll be late for school."

Grandma's head shot up. "Why you heading away from the schoolhouse then, missy?"

Lucy shifted uncomfortably. "I'm having breakfast with the Rosseters," she said.

Grandma Brazee laughed again. "That's it, girl," she cried as Lucy made her way back toward the road. "You make nice with Jesse's family. That's the way to do it."

Lucy's face flushed. She wished everyone would just shut up about her and Jesse.

Lucy hurried down the road toward the Rosseter house, passing mountain houses and barns along the way. She could hear the sounds of plates clinking against each other, water running, heavy boots on wooden floors, pigs snorting, a rooster crowing a late morning call. Next to the lower lake, cows stood in the meadow. One cow let out a low moo, crying for her morning milking.

Lucy saw old Ezekiel Johanson walking toward the cows, swinging a bucket and whistling. He had been on the mountain as long as Lucy had been there, but he did not work the blast furnace. He was a Swiss farmer who liked the remoteness of the community and the guaranteed market of those who needed his flax, wheat, and potatoes. Mr. Johanson had never married, but he knew every child on the mountain and had whittled each of them a small wooden cow at their birth.

"Hey, Lucy," he called.

"Hello, Mr. Johanson," she called back.

"Sorry about yer whipping last night," he said. "Hope yer all right today."

Lucy just nodded. How had *he* managed to hear about it too? Grandma Brazee must have been very busy this morning spreading the story. Now Lucy wished she had put a dead mouse in the crazy woman's sewing basket after all. The old gossip deserved it!

Lucy opened the wooden gate that protected the Rosseters' herb gardens, and saw Jesse's four-year-old sister, Annie, playing in the front yard.

"Lucy!" Annie jumped to her feet and ran to hug Lucy.

"Hey, Annie," Lucy said. "You already finished your breakfast?"

"It's too loud in there," Annie complained. "I'll eat when everyone's gone."

Lucy laughed. "Is Jess inside?"

Annie shook her head. "No. He's gone to the furnace today. He and Pa had a terrible argument this morning. Jess wanted to go to school, but Pa said it's time he started to work, being fifteen now and all. Jesse stormed out, and they ain't talking."

So Jesse wouldn't be at school for this last week of classes? Although most of the boys quit school permanently around Jesse's age to begin working the iron, they usually finished out the school year. Lucy was stunned. She hadn't anticipated this.

The front door opened, and Mrs. Rosseter stepped out onto the porch. "Lucy," she said, "you come by for Jesse? He ain't here."

"Annie told me," Lucy said, hearing the bleakness in her own voice.

"Well, I still welcome your company, Lucy," Mrs. Rosseter said. "I hope you know that. You had breakfast?"

Lucy shook her head. "No," she said. "Father had to go down off."

Mrs. Rosseter waved her toward the house. "Come on in, then. We're all just finishing up." She glanced at Annie. "And you, young miss. You come and eat now. I don't plan on making more breakfast later."

"Aw, Ma," Annie complained. "It's too noisy for me."

"Be worse if it's too silent, like it's gonna be in a few minutes," Mrs. Rosseter said. "'Cause when it's quiet, that means everyone's gone. I'll be working on something else, and it won't be your breakfast. So if you ain't planning on going hungry this morning, you'd best get inside and eat."

Annie grabbed Lucy's hand. "Sit with me?" she asked.

Lucy smiled. "There's nothing I'd like better," she said.

And they climbed the stairs to the Rosseters' kitchen.

4.

Inside the Rosseters' house, the Franklin stove was blazing, warming the room and sending out a comforting glow. Three of Jesse's brothers and sisters, along with Jesse's grandpa, sat eating at the long wooden table that seated all ten of the Rosseters when they ate together. Jesse's siblings all yelled their hellos to Lucy and begged her to sit next to them. But first Lucy went to the front of the table so that Jesse's grandpa could see her. The old man was hard of hearing.

"Hello, Grandpa," Lucy said loudly, touching his shoulder.

The old man grinned. "Hey, Lucy," he shouted. "Take a seat."

Lucy smiled. She loved Grandpa Rosseter, even if he did yell. He just had no idea how loud his voice was. He had lost most of his hearing at the age of forty, after too many years in the mountain forge, standing inside the building where the fires raged and the water-powered metal hammer rose up and down, up and down, crashing over and over into the iron that had come from the furnace. The hammer beat out the iron's impurities and most of Grandpa's hearing in the process.

Lucy took a seat next to Annie as she'd promised. Mary, who was eight, began to pout.

"You want some breakfast?" Grandpa shouted, pushing a bowl of oatmeal toward her.

Lucy smiled and nodded her thanks. Then she dug in. She loved eating here. She loved the chaos of this place, Grandpa's shouting, and the sound of all Jesse's brothers and sisters arguing. The confusion drove Jesse mad. But for Lucy, being alone was a daily given, and Jesse's family made her feel alive.

Mr. Rosseter came into the kitchen, buttoning his shirt.

"Lucy," he said gruffly.

"Hello, Mr. Rosseter," Lucy said.

Of all Jesse's family, Mr. Rosseter was the one

Lucy knew the least. He was a hardworking man, spending long hours at the furnace, or with his animals and fields when the blast furnace shut down in the fall. He wasn't around much when Lucy came to visit, and when he was there, he was a quiet man, taken to reading or repairing things in their house.

Mrs. Rosseter came to the table, baby Polly on her hip. She handed the baby to Grandpa.

"You want some coffee, Luce?" she asked.

"Sure," Lucy said.

Mrs. Rosseter poured coffee into a tin cup and put it in front of Lucy. Then she reached into a basket by the door, drew out some sewing, and came to sit with the rest of them.

"I'm going," Mr. Rosseter said. He bent to kiss his wife. "Jesse best be at the furnace when I get there."

"He will be," Mrs. Rosseter assured him softly. "He may not think he wants to do that kind of work, but he's an obedient son."

Mr. Rosseter's eyes suddenly hardened. "I don't understand him," he said, his voice rising, becoming sharp as metal. "It's a good life, working the iron up here. It's made us all a decent living."

The Rosseter children paused, some were chewing, some held spoons halfway to their mouths. Lucy held her breath. She had heard about Mr. Rosseter's anger from Jesse, but she herself had never seen Mr. Rosseter mad, nor had she ever heard him raise his voice like he was doing now. She felt uncomfortable sitting there in the middle of it.

Mrs. Rosseter clicked her tongue. "I know. You said so earlier, but don't go getting all upset again."

"The boy should be more grateful," Jesse's father said, shaking his head, his voice dropping a notch. "He ain't got no idea what it's like to be poor, to not know where your next meal is coming from."

Mrs. Rosseter smiled. "He's a boy, and that's all," she said, poking a strand of thread through her needle.

Mr. Rosseter pulled up his suspenders and snapped them on his shoulders. "A boy who's a man now," he said. "A boy who should be done with those foolish dreams of his."

Mrs. Rosseter reached up and touched her husband's waist, making him glance down at her. "Every boy dreams. You did too. I remember."

Mr. Rosseter paused for a moment, nodding at Grandpa. “He dreamed of coming here, dreamed of a better life for us than we had back in Latvia.”

“And it is a better life,” Mrs. Rosseter said, rising and kissing her husband on the cheek. “Stop fussing about it now. It’ll work out. Jesse’ll understand why you’re doing this someday. Now off with you, or you’ll be late for your shift at the furnace.”

Mr. Rosseter nodded, picked up his hat, and was gone. Mrs. Rosseter sat back down and started sewing, and the kids began eating again. The house itself seemed to draw a fresh breath with his leaving.

“Jess ain’t gonna go to school anymore, Lucy,” explained Sadie, who was thirteen.

“So I heard,” Lucy said.

“He and Pa had an awful argument this morning,” Mary spoke up. “Jesse wanted to finish up the school year, but Pa said there weren’t no reason for Jesse to go to school now that he could work at the ironworks. Jess yelled back how he hated the furnace and the forges, and especially the charcoal pits.”

“That’s enough, Mary,” Mrs. Rosseter said. “No need to air dirty linen.”

Lucy's stomach turned. So that was where he was to start out—learning to be a collier, making charcoal for the furnace. It was a filthy, tiring job, and Lucy knew Jesse would be doubly unhappy with his first assignment. Not that he would have welcomed a job at the furnace with his father, or at one of the forges that Grandpa had worked either.

"You want down?" Grandpa shouted at baby Polly who was fussing. Polly's eyes widened at Grandpa's loud voice. She began to cry, and Grandpa, who seemed unaware that he had caused the baby to be upset, looked at Mrs. Rosseter helplessly.

"Oh, be quiet, Polly," Sadie said irritably.

"That's enough, Sadie," Mrs. Rosseter said as she lifted the baby from Grandpa's arms and set her down on the floor with a wooden rattle to chew on.

Lucy drank her coffee and finished her oatmeal, their warmth filling her stomach, but she couldn't get Jesse out of her mind. "You don't think Jess will do something foolish, do you, Mrs. Rosseter?" she couldn't help asking.

"Oh, he's all right," Sadie said, and sniffed. "He's

just gonna go to work. I don't know why he complains about it. Joseph don't mind."

Joseph was Jesse's older brother, who had already worked three seasons at the furnace. He had become quite skilled at mixing ore, lime, and charcoal in just the right proportions and then adding it to the furnace to produce iron.

"Jess wants to be a navy captain," Mary boasted. "He told me. He's gonna come back here looking just as fine as them navy captains from Washington, D.C., with their brass buttons and all."

Mrs. Rosseter shook her head. "Let's not say things like that in front of your pa, Mary."

"Pa's not here," Mary pointed out.

"Don't get smart, missy," Mrs. Rosseter said. "You want some more oatmeal, Lucy?"

Lucy nodded, and Mrs. Rosseter spooned more of the hot cereal from a large iron pot into her bowl. "Don't worry about Jesse," Mrs. Rosseter said, smiling at Lucy. "His pa just wants the best for him, and he believes working on this mountain is the answer. Jesse and his pa will work this out."

"Heading on out to the outhouse," Grandpa yelled.

"Jeesh," Sadie said. "Does he gotta shout it out?"

"He can't hear well, Sadie," Mary pointed out.

"I know that," Sadie snapped.

Lucy chuckled at Jesse's sisters' squabbling as she helped Grandpa push himself up from the table and watched as he hobbled out the back door toward the privy.

Daniel, Jesse's two-year-old brother, struggled to get onto the table to reach some corn bread.

"Hungry," he said.

Mrs. Rosseter stood up and handed Daniel a piece of the bread, pushing him back into his chair. Daniel stuck the whole thing in his mouth, letting the crumbs spill onto the table and the floor. Mrs. Rosseter sighed and got a broom to sweep up the food.

"Hungry," Daniel repeated when he was done with the first piece.

"No more," Mrs. Rosseter said sternly.

Daniel climbed down from his chair and tottered over to Lucy. "Hungry, Lu," he said to her.

Lucy smiled at his chubby form. She picked him up and gave him a cuddle. "You heard your ma," she said.

"No more now, or you'll be too big for your britches."

Daniel squirmed from her grasp and wiggled to the floor. He went over and took the wooden rattle from Polly's hands. Polly began to cry again.

"Honestly," Mrs. Rosseter said in exasperation. "I don't know how I get anything done. Speaking of which, at least three of you had best skedaddle and get to the schoolhouse, or you're gonna be late."

"Thanks for breakfast, Mrs. Rosseter," Lucy said, pushing back her chair.

Mrs. Rosseter picked up Polly to quiet her. "You're mighty welcome, Lucy. And don't worry. Jesse'll make his peace with his pa, or they'll find another path."

Then she turned toward the girls. "Sadie, Mary, let's go. Walk on with Lucy now." She sighed. "Then maybe, just maybe, I can get some real work done around here."

Daniel tottered over to his mother. He threw his arms around her legs. "Hungry," he said.

Grandpa called for help from the outhouse.

"Then again," Mrs. Rosseter said, laughing slightly, "maybe not."

Lucy laughed with her, then ran with Sadie and Mary up the hill toward the schoolhouse.

A fire was blazing inside, and after the chilly run, Lucy welcomed the warmth. Everyone was in a celebratory mood. This was the last week of school before the recess, and although everyone knew that they would be working hard in the fields or at home until mid-October, the break meant a welcome change of pace.

Lucy took her seat on the wooden bench nearest the fire. Her father had more time than other parents to provide the schoolhouse with a large supply of firewood, and this meant Lucy got a seat near the stove and stayed warm most of the winter. She felt sorry for the children whose parents didn't have the time to gather as much wood. They had to sit farther from the fire, and often caught cold. Lucy's father said that in other towns only the wealthy children sat near the fire, as their parents paid for firewood. Up on the mountain, though, it wasn't a question of money.

Her throat closed as she sat down, thinking of

how just last week Jesse had been sitting two rows behind her, trying to hit her with spitballs. Lucy knew that when a boy started work at the furnace, he left the classroom for good. Still, she wished that Mr. Rosseter had seen his way to letting Jesse come for the last week of school, even if it was the beginning of the iron season.

There were two other girls her age on the mountain, Julia Bishop and Betsy Sherwood. They were best friends and rarely left each other's side. When Jesse had been there, this hadn't bothered Lucy, but now, seeing the two of them with their heads together, Lucy felt the loss of Jesse even more deeply.

"Master Griggs is coming!" someone shouted from the window.

Everyone hurried to get in their seats and get their primers out. Master Griggs was not known for sparing his ruler on students' knuckles, even if it was the last week of school.

And so the day passed slowly. Lucy worked on her arithmetic and tried hard not to think about Jesse. When at last school was out, Lucy rose stiffly from the hard bench and ran with the others out into the spring sunshine.

The sound of the furnace roared above the giggles of the children. Some of the younger ones waved for Lucy to follow them to the green for some games and fun, but she pretended not to see them. Instead she slipped as quietly as she could away from the schoolhouse and down the road toward the furnace.

She knew she'd be in trouble if she were caught. Girls weren't allowed near the ironworks, but she couldn't help herself. She had to go.

She scurried around the edge of the lake. The furnace, which was but a few hundred yards beyond the dam at the end of the lower lake, roared in her ears. The men were working hard, hauling limestone and charcoal and iron ore to the opening at the top of the furnace. A pipe that vented the poisonous gases created by the process of producing iron threw flames and sparks high into the air. Lucy could hear the sound of the forges farther down the stream, the sharp clanging of metal on metal as iron was bent into shape. Lucy didn't want to be seen, but she needn't have worried. Everyone was so busy, they took no note of her, and she slid past easily, climbing the short distance to the meadow where the colliers worked. Here they kept a low fire burning, making the charcoal that was necessary for mixing with the iron ore and limestone to produce molten metal.

When the colliers came into sight at last, Lucy slipped quietly behind a tree at the edge of the clearing. Carefully she skirted the meadow where large charcoal stacks burned in huge hills. Then she saw Jesse, dirty and sweaty, up on a ladder that leaned against one of the charcoal piles.

"No, no, no," Charles Jorgen shouted up at Jesse in his heavy Swedish accent. "Ya cannot make the charcoal without the patience. Ya must keep the fire going, but it must not get too hot. Too hot, all the wood burns and nothing is left. Not hot enough, ya have no fire to make the charcoal. Concentrate, boy. Concentrate."

He handed Jesse a long stick.

"Go on." He indicated with his hand. "The fire needs some air, boy. Can't ya see it needs a little space?"

Jesse took the pole from Charles. He poked

unhappily at the dirt and sod that covered the smoldering fire. A part of the dirt fell in, and flames shot out. The fire roared.

"No, no," Charles said, rushing to throw sod up to Jesse so he could smother the large flames and get the hill smoldering softly again. "I tell ya again, boy, yer too impatient. Don't just poke. Ya must work the fire. It is like clay, boy. Ya must mold the charcoal."

Jesse let out a loud sigh, and as he did, his eyes met Lucy's. She stared at him.

"Yer attitude is not good, Jesse Rosseter," Charles said disgustedly. "Ya may not be fit to do the ironwork. I do not know what yer papa will do with ya then."

Jesse's eyes left Lucy's, but not before she had seen the anger in them. Jesse grabbed the pole and stuck it into the sod and dirt again.

"What are ya doing?" Charles shouted out. He grabbed the pole from Jesse.

Lucy couldn't bear to watch anymore, and she ran from the meadow. It was unfair. Why did life have to change? Why did Jesse have to quit school and do something he hated? Why did her father think she should leave the mountain to marry into a life she would probably hate too? Why couldn't she and Jesse be as they always had been?

Lucy didn't want to grow up yet, and she didn't want Jesse to either!

5.

Lucy hurried to the store after leaving the meadow. When her father was off the mountain, she was expected to go to the shop in the afternoons and help out. The bell above the shop door gave off a high, tinkling sound. Eric Moseman, her father's assistant from New York City, came out from the back room.

"Master Griggs keep you a little later than usual?" he asked gruffly.

Lucy's face grew warm.

"You know you're not to be near the furnace, Lucy," Mr. Moseman said, but his voice was kind.

"I know," Lucy muttered.

Mr. Moseman laughed. "Just be glad that I was here, and not your father. He wants you here directly after school, remember?"

Lucy sighed. "Yes, I remember."

Mr. Moseman nodded. "Good. Then, if you'll mind the store, I'll go in back and do the rest of the inventory before your father arrives with that new shipment. All right?"

Lucy nodded and went behind the wooden counter. She knew Mr. Moseman wasn't doing inventory but instead was probably drinking a little hard cider, swapping stories, and playing checkers with one of his old cronies. She found one of the store aprons and tied it around her waist. Then she sat and waited.

Lucy heard Mr. Moseman laugh a bit, and the voice of Abram Ostrander, Ezra Ostrander's brother, talking in low tones. *Probably discussing my whipping*, she thought sourly.

Still, Lucy didn't blame Mr. Moseman or the others for gathering at her father's store to gossip. Mail came here once a week, and it was one of the few places on the mountain where men could come occasionally to socialize and have a good stiff drink.

Plus, being a shopkeeper was such a dull job. Unless someone came to buy something, there was nothing to do except stock the shelves, sweep the floor, and count the money. Since Mr. Moseman did most of these things himself, when Lucy watched the store, there was truly nothing at all to do. She stared at the cloth bolts, the iron nails, the bonnets from France, the barrels of flour. She sighed.

The bell on the front door tinkled. Jesse's older brother, Joseph, came tripping into the store along with Jenny Sims. The two had their arms about each other and were laughing at something. They stood like that until Lucy cleared her throat loudly.

Joseph smiled when he saw Lucy. "Hey there, Luce," he said. "Yer pa down off?"

Lucy nodded. "Did you finish your shift?" she asked, noticing his grimy face and hands.

"Sure have," Joseph said, and nodded. "And a good first day it was too."

Jenny giggled.

"Can I get you something?" Lucy said, trying to be polite and to keep the disgust from her voice. The two of them acted as if nothing else in this world existed except each other.

"Just wanted to buy Miss Sims here a little candy,"

Joseph said, "to celebrate the furnace being up and running today. A new beginning for a new year." He grinned at Jenny. "1820 is gonna be the best year ever, ain't it, Miss Sims?"

Jenny Sims nodded and blushed.

Lucy thought she might be sick. "Well, what do you want, then?" she asked irritably. "I've got a lot to do."

"Oh," Joseph said. "Sorry. What would you like, Miss Sims?"

Jenny still didn't speak but simply pointed to some licorice whips displayed in the glass case. Lucy wondered for the umpteenth time if Jenny even had a voice or if she had been blessed simply with giggles and the ability to blush.

Slowly, Lucy filled a brown paper bag with the candy. She handed it to Jenny and then turned toward Joseph. "You want anything?"

Joseph shook his head and handed Lucy some coins. "Nah," he said. "I got what I want already."

He slipped his arm around Jenny's waist, making her giggle again and making Lucy wish they'd go outside.

"Well, we'll be seeing you, Luce," Joseph said as they started for the door. "You should stop by later, come hear how Jesse's first day was."

Lucy nodded, though she already knew how his first day had been. Outside, Lucy heard the jingle of a harness and the creaking of wagon wheels coming to a stop. Joseph pulled open the shop door just as Lucy's father was about to enter.

"Joseph," Lucy's father said, his voice loud and hearty, "I understand congratulations are in order for you and Miss Sims here."

Lucy stared at them. Joseph was the one blushing now.

"Heard you were accepted this very day," Lucy's father continued. "Just saw your pa, and he told me. He's very proud of you, son. You're a fine iron-worker, and I'm sure you'll be a fine husband, too. Congratulations."

"Thank you, sir," Joseph said. "I guess if you've already heard, I should be going to let Ma know. I saw Pa at the furnace just as I was leaving, but I haven't had a chance to tell Ma yet."

"Well then, son," Lucy's father said, "you'd better

go quickly. Good news like that travels fast in this community."

"Yes, sir," Joseph said. "Thank you, Mr. Pettee." Joseph ran from the store, pulling Jenny after him.

Lucy watched them leave, her mouth agape. Joseph was getting married! And Jenny Sims would be Jesse's sister-in-law! Lucy thought of all the times she and Jesse had laughed themselves silly over Jenny's inability to do anything but giggle. Now Jesse would have to endure all that giggling—permanently!

Lucy couldn't help but smile at the thought. She itched to find Jesse and tease him about it. Working up at the charcoal pits meant he probably hadn't heard the news yet.

Her father walked into the shop. "How was school today, Luce?"

"Fine," Lucy said. "Can I go home now?"

Lucy knew she didn't have to begin preparing supper for an hour or so, and maybe Jesse would be finished at the charcoal pits by now and at one of their favorite spots on the mountain. If she found him, then she could be the first to tell him about his brother and Jenny and get to enjoy his shock.

"Sure," her father said. "In fact, I'll walk with you."

"Eric," her father called.

Mr. Moseman came out from the back of the store. "Get some good things, Jonathan?" he asked.

"Plenty. It's all out in the wagon," Lucy's father said. "And it looks like I'll be bringing a wedding dress up too. Joseph Rosseter and Jenny Sims are to tie the knot."

Mr. Moseman grinned. "'It's about timc," he said. "Any other news from down off?"

Lucy's father nodded. "Alice Ball's just had herself a baby girl in New York. I'm going on up to tell Charlotte in a bit."

Mr. Moseman nodded. "That's good news. I know Charlotte's missed her sister something fierce since she left with that navy man."

Lucy's father nodded. "Luckily that docsn't happen too often. I'm going to walk Lucy home before I head up to Charlotte's. I've got a little something at home that I bought for Lucy. Then I'll be back. You all right here?"

Mr. Moseman grinned. "I just beat Abram three games to one. With the wager we made on each game, I suspect he's ready to head home now, and I can be out front."

Lucy's father chuckled. "Don't relieve him of too much hard-earned money, Eric, or he won't have any left to spend in the store. Let's go, Luce."

Lucy followed her father out of the shop, her mind now preoccupied. She had forgotten about the present. Though she was disappointed about not having some time to find Jesse and give him the wonderful news about Jenny Sims, she was curious about what her father might have gotten her.

She walked with him past the wagon, fully loaded with things for the store. A tarp covered the items and was tied fast with rope to hold it in place during the long journey up the mountain road. Behind the wagon, Lucy saw an empty second cart. The horse that had drawn the wagon and cart was still breathing heavily.

When they got to the house, her father stopped her. "Come on up the steps," he said. "But when we get to the front door, I want you to close your eyes. The surprise is in the parlor."

Lucy smiled. What was it? What had he gotten

her? She climbed the porch steps excitedly, then obediently shut her eyes. Her father took her hand. She heard the front door open, and she let him lead her over the threshold and into their house. Then he steered her into thc parlor.

"All right," he said. "You can open your eyes now."

In front of Lucy lay a new wooden spinet.

"Father," Lucy breathed, "it's beautiful! But why would you get that for me? I don't play."

"A man from down off will be coming up once a week to give you lessons," her father said. "I know I haven't given you many of the social graces you'll need to take your place in good society, Luce, but piano playing is a start. Do you like it?"

Lucy stared at the instrument. It was pretty, all glossy and new. She went over and ran her fingers over the keys. It gave off a nice sound. But would she like lessons? Would she be happy inside on a warm June day listening to some man tell her how to play? Her father would want her to practice. That would mean more time inside. And playing the spinet would mean she was one step closer to having social graces, which would mean leaving the mountain and entering into that awful state of marriage.

Her father was smiling, his face full of love for her. She couldn't bear to disappoint him.

"Yes, Father," she said. "It will be fun, I'm sure."

He came over and gave her a hug. "I knew you'd like it. I also hired a painter to do your portrait," he said. "He'll be coming along with the teacher this summer, and you can sit for him after your lesson. All the refined ladies are having their portraits done these days."

Lucy sighed. Sit for a lesson on the spinet, then sit while someone painted her portrait? How could she possibly spend all that time sitting? It seemed acquiring social graces was a tedious task.

"I've got to get the rest of that wagon unloaded and go give the good news to Charlotte Ball," her father said, finally pulling away. He smiled at her as he went to pick up his hat off the horsehair sofa.

"I'm thinking that if you get good enough at playing, there'll be plenty of folks up here who will want to buy a spinet for themselves, too," he said. "That will be good for business."

He motioned toward the instrument. "Go ahead, Lucy," he said. "Sit down and give it a try. I'll be excited to hear what you think when I get back for supper."

Dutifully, Lucy sat down at the spinet. She placed her hands on the keys and tapped at them.

"You're a natural," her father said. "I knew you would be."

Lucy forced a smile.

"All right, then," her father said. "I'd better get to work."

Lucy watched him go and then stared at the spinet. Already her legs were itching to stand up and run off. She hit the keys a few more times, and then could do it no longer. She stood and crept to the door. Her father was walking down the hill. She waited until he had rounded the bend, then grabbed up her shawl and headed out, up into the mountain.

6.

Laurel was blooming in abundance, and Lucy stopped to pick a few sprigs to take home. If anyone saw her hurrying past the lower lake toward the upper lake and the cliff, she would have an excuse for not being at home doing her chores. Besides, the mountain laurel would look pretty on the table at suppertime.

Her breath came in quick gasps as she walked up the long, hard mountain path. She waved to William Merritt, who ran the sawmill between the two lakes. He was a Yankee who had come to the mountain a few years back when the mountain folk decided to start the sawmill and send the lumber down off. He nodded to Lucy, pausing as he lifted finished boards into a large stack.

Even with the sound of the sawmill and the furnace and forges running, it was quieter up here.

The monsters still roared, but the sound was distant. Sometimes, when she was high on the upper lake, she felt as if she had entered another world.

She found the path she and Jesse had worn down to a bit of rock, which jutted out into the surface of the water—the Old Landing they called it. There they could sit and see other mountains far off in the distance, and watch the beavers build a dam up near the source of both the upper and lower lakes.

Lucy walked down the path, then stopped when she heard a noise. It could have been just a bird, or even a snake winding through the grass. But in rare instances, she had surprised a bear.

Lucy listened hard until the noise became more rhythmic. Then she grinned and scurried down the path.

Jesse didn't even look up from his whittling. "Hey," he said. He was sooty and disheveled, but Lucy had never been so glad to see anyone in her life.

"Hello yourself," she said, and went to sit next to him. "Hard day?" she asked as she settled her skirts around her.

"You making a joke?" he asked.

Lucy grinned, but Jesse did not smile back.

She watched him whittle a minute more. Then as casually as she could, she asked, "Been home yet?"

Jesse looked at her as if she were crazy. "Do I look like I been home?" he asked. "You know my ma. Do you reckon she'd let me near the inside of the house, covered in soot?"

Lucy could hardly surpress a giggle, knowing about Jenny Sims and Jesse's brother.

"What's so funny?" Jesse asked. "You mocking the way I look? That ain't kind, Lucy, considering how much I hated today."

Lucy's giggle froze in her throat. She coughed. "I'm sorry," she said. "It wasn't that."

"What, then?" Jesse asked, scowling.

Jesse's unhappiness with work was lingering longer than she had suspected it would, even here by the upper lake, where his bad moods usually vanished. She wondered if it was to be like this every day now for Jesse.

"Was it that awful?" she asked him softly.

"No," he said sourly. "It was worse."

Lucy stared out at the water. The sun was dipping

low, casting its rays across the lake. There was a tiny splash beside her, and Jesse was at the water's edge, casting off the small boat he had finished whittling. Lucy rose and went to stand beside him, watching the wooden boat rock back and forth on the water.

Jesse sighed. "Why won't he let me just join the navy like I want? Why does he always tell me I'm weak in the head for wanting that?"

There was nothing for Lucy to say to this. They had talked for hours about Jesse's father's refusal to acknowledge his son's dream, a dream Jesse had nurtured since he had been little and first seen the navy men come to the mountain. The navy men had told him stories of the sea, and Jesse had been enchanted ever since.

But Lucy thought she understood Jesse's father just a little too. All of the workers on the mountain who worked the furnace had come here from overseas, from places like Lithuania, Latvia, Switzerland, and Sweden. They were grateful to have food, a place to live, and money to spend, and they were proud of their traditions. Most families stayed, each generation working the furnace, each family watching the next marry and have babies. Jesse was one of the few who had even dared to think of a life off of the mountain.

"I just want to be on the water," Jesse said. "I just want to sail across oceans, see far-off lands. I don't want to be an ironworker, stuck in all this noise and dirt. What's so wrong with that?"

Lucy repeated what she'd said in the past. "I know you want to join the navy, but it's dangerous, Jess. Lots of ships these days are being captured by the British, and the sailors on board are forced to work for them. It's damp and dark on those boats. The spaces are small, and there are rats. The food is horrible. So maybe the furnace is better work, Jess. At least here, you're out in the air. At least you're on the mountain. At least you're safe. Maybe your pa is right that a life so filled with uncertainties is no life at all."

Jesse laughed bitterly. He held up his sooty hands. "This is better? Spending my days making charcoal? Or working hours pushing them wheelbarrows of limestone and ore to the top of the furnace, breaking my back? Or catching the iron when it pours out below, hoping against hope not to burn myself someday? Or maybe I should work at the forge buildings and eventually go nearly deaf like my grandpa? That sound like a good life to you?"

"It's not that bad," Lucy said angrily.

"Aw, you just love this old place," Jesse muttered.

Lucy stared at him. She hated the fact that Jesse had to do what he was doing, but enough was enough. They had talked this whole situation over so many times, she could predict what each of them would say next. She grabbed Jesse by the shoulders.

"Well now, Jesse Rosseter," she snapped, "you're right about that. I do love this mountain. And I'm tired of listening to your talk about leaving it and leaving me. You're so sour today that I have half a mind to go practice that old spinet my father has just bought me, so I can learn good social graces and marry well and leave *you* behind!"

"Marry?" Jesse said, his eyes widening. He sat down abruptly.

"Yes," Lucy said sourly, sitting down next to him. "That's what my father wants *me* to do. So, you have to work the iron. Maybe you'd prefer to marry some man you don't even know so you can clean and cook and sew for him? Does that sound better?"

Jesse was laughing now. The irritable mood seemed to have suddenly flown from him. "Who do you think's gonna marry you, Luce? You're skinny as a chicken, and the last time I ate at your house, it weren't much to speak of. And as for your sewing, as I recall, your sampler was basically a bunch of knots. No, Lucy Pettee, there ain't no one who would marry you."

He grinned and threw an arm around her waist, pulling her to him. "Except for me, maybe."

Lucy paused. Was he serious?

Then Jesse began to tickle her sides, and Lucy fell back, trying to escape him. She wiggled and squirmed, attempting to free herself, laughing at the familiarity of it all. Her heart lifted to see him happy and teasing her again.

Jesse smiled down at her, and in that moment, Lucy felt the world suddenly stop. Jesse's dancing eyes were green as new spring grass, and his wide smile was warm and magical as summer sunshine. How had she not seen this before? She shivered.

Jesse released her and sat back up. "Of course, I'd only marry you 'cause Pa says I'm weak in the head, remember?" He laughed again.

Lucy sat up too, feeling shaky. What had she just been thinking? This was Jesse, just Jesse her friend, laughing and teasing her as he had done for years.

She took a deep breath in an effort to slow her heart. The world tipped and righted itself.

"That Jenny Sims, though, now there's a real catch," Lucy said, her voice thick.

"Jenny Sims," Jesse guffawed, picking up a stick and throwing it out into the water. "That little ninny who can't say a word but just giggles and giggles? Who'd ever marry her?"

"Your brother," Lucy said, smiling with relief at feeling normal again.

Jesse snorted. "My brother wouldn't marry her. He just courts her for something to do. He told me."

Lucy grinned. "Well, he must have wanted to throw you off his tracks, Jess, because he came into the shop today, and my father told him congratulations on his upcoming marriage to none other than Miss Jenny Sims. And your brother thanked him kindly."

Jesse stared at her, horrified. "No," he said. "He wouldn't. Not my brother. He's too smart."

Lucy laughed, stood up, and began to head back up the path. Now that things with Jesse were right again and she had given him the news she had come to deliver, she knew she had better get home before her father caught her avoiding her chores again.

"So," she said, bending to pick up her mountain laurel, "I guess Jenny will be living at the Rosseter home, giggling her way through all your meals."

"Aw," Jesse said, kicking out at a rock. "What'd Joe go and do that for?

"Wait," he yelled out, seeing her heading away from him, "where you going?"

"Home," she said, "to practice my spinet, so I don't have to marry someone who's weak in the head like you."

She flounced halfway up the path and then turned to grin down at him one more time. "And you'd better hurry on home too, Jess," she said. "You don't want to miss that first meal with Jenny Sims."

Jesse threw a stone after her, and Lucy laughed as she gathered up her skirts and ran home to make supper for her father.

7.

"Please, Miss Pettee," Arthur complained, "if you keep moving like that, I will never get it right."

Lucy tried her best to keep still, but it was such a hot August day that sitting having her portrait painted was unbearable. Lucy almost wished she could be working the iron instead. At least at the furnace and forges, she could run back and forth with a wheelbarrow, or draw forms in the sand for the iron, or swing a hammer. Sitting still while this artist painted her was impossible. The hot summer heat melted its way into the shaded house and sent rivulets of sweat down the side of her face. She wanted a lemonade and a fan.

An itch began on her nose. Lucy twitched, trying to keep her hands still in her lap. The itch did not go away. She wiggled her nose, up and down, up and down. The tickle was driving her mad. Finally she could stand it no longer. She lifted a hand and furiously scratched.

"Ach," the artist yelled, throwing down his brushes. "This is an impossible task you make for me, Miss Pettee."

Her father came into the room with a tin cup of coffee. "Problems?" he asked mildly, but there were the beginnings of a smile on his face.

"Your daughter, sir," the artist huffed, "is a poor subject for a portrait. She does not know the proper way to sit still. I am in great difficulty of capturing her on the canvas. You must tell her not to move."

The grin that had threatened to show on her father's face broke through.

"My dear Arthur," her father said to the Lithuanian painter, "telling Lucy to sit still is like telling a bird to stay on one branch. It will never happen. And why should it? Would you like a woman who has so little enthusiasm for life that she could simply sit for hours without moving?" Her father shook his head. "No, Arthur," he said, "give me a woman with high amounts of energy. She will keep a house properly and still have something left over. Besides, when I see Lucy like this, she reminds me of her mother."

"I do?" Lucy asked, feeling her face flush. Her father so rarely spoke of her mother.

Lucy's father nodded. "Yes, Luce," he said, "your mother was high-spirited, like you. She was a woman who accomplished much in her day."

The artist gathered up his brushes. "Still, Mr. Pettee," he said, "I am afraid this portrait may take longer than I had originally anticipated. I am hoping this will not be a problem for you."

Her father shook his head. "No, Arthur," he said. "We aren't in a hurry."

Lucy nodded. She hoped the portrait would be *very* long in the making, even if it did mean sitting still for hours. The more time it took, the longer it would be until her father made the next step concerning Lucy's future off the mountain.

"Lucy," her father said, "take a break now and get Arthur here some coffee, won't you?"

Lucy gladly left the mahogany side chair she had been made to sit upon. She stretched luxuriously as she moved toward the kitchen. The Franklin stove was burning slowly and a hot pot of coffee was warm on the back burner. Lucy lifted it.

A face suddenly appeared at the window, causing her to almost drop the pot. She let out a scream. The back door opened, and Jesse poked his sooty face in.

"Lucy?" her father called. "You all right?"

Jesse held a finger to his lips to quiet her.

"I'm fine, Father," she called. "I just thought I saw a mouse."

"What are you doing here?" she hissed at Jesse. "Aren't you supposed to be at the charcoal pits?"

"'Course I am," he whispered back. "But I come to tell you something. There are rumors around that old Ezekiel Johanson saw that Tory ghost last night when he was out checking on his cows. A bunch of us are gonna go to the graveyard tomorrow night to see if we can spot him."

A shiver ran down Lucy's spine. She hated the story of the Tory who had been hanged up on the mountain as he'd tried to flee the colonists during the Revolutionary War. It spooked her to walk past that tree near the graveyard where they said he had met his death. His ghost wasn't seen often, maybe once every twenty years or so, but she didn't like to think that Mr. Johanson had seen him so recently.

"You know Mr. Johanson is old," she said. "Maybe he mistook one of his cows for a ghost."

Jesse grinned. "Scared, Luce?"

"No," she said angrily. "Just realistic. That man is always telling tall tales."

"Well, this tale was the same as them others," Jesse said. "The Tory approached him, holding out his hands, and his neck was all bloody."

Lucy shivered again. "We've all heard that story a million times," she said. "It would be easy for him to tell it to you."

"Coming or not, Luce?" Jesse asked, ignoring her.

"Father wouldn't let me," Lucy said.

"Never known that to stop you before," Jesse said mildly. "Many's the night you've shimmied down that honeysuckle trellis to take a late-night swim with me."

Lucy was trapped. Jesse was smiling that wide, slow easy grin he had, the one that challenged her, the one that got her in trouble every time, the one she secretly loved because she knew it meant they were going to have an adventure. And Lord knew it had been some time since they'd had one. Over the past three months, Lucy had barely even seen Jesse, as spring had slipped into the height of summer. Jesse had been busy at the furnace, working from sunup to sundown. As for Lucy, she had been occupied with portrait painting, piano practicing, the summer canning of vegetables and fruits, and the tending of their garden—most of the same chores that other children her age did during the summer break from school.

"What time?" she said.

"'Bout midnight," Jesse said. "Best time for catching ghosts, they say. But then, maybe that's not your style, Lucy Pettee."

"I'll be there," Lucy retorted. "I just hope that ghost eats you alive when I send him your way."

She picked up the coffeepot and swept off toward the parlor. But she could hear Jesse laughing softly behind her, and she wished that she'd thought it through just a little more before she had agreed to go.

8.

The next night, Lucy lay in bed, jiggling her legs furiously under the covers. Her eyes threatened to close. She bounced her legs around again, trying desperately to stay awake until midnight.

A small ping sounded on the glass of her window. Lucy jumped from her bed and looked outside. The light from the blast furnace lit their front yard as if it were early evening and not nearly midnight. Clouds scuttled about overhead, letting a small slice of moonlight peek out every now and then.

"Come on," came a whispered voice from below the window.

"You're early," Lucy hissed back, wondering if he could hear her above the noise of the furnace. She could barely hear him.

"Don't matter," Jesse said. "Come on. They're all waiting by the edge of the wood."

Lucy had lain fully dressed in bed. So she simply swung her legs over the windowsill, caught the edge of the trellis and hand over hand, climbed her way down. The summer night air was warm and soft.

Jesse grinned when she reached the bottom. He spit on his hand and held it to hers. She spit and rubbed her palm against his, feeling reassured by their old ritual. Then he grabbed her hand, and they ran for the woods along the road.

At the edge of the trees, in the dark, Julia Bishop and Betsy Sherwood waited for them. Joseph was there with Sadie, too. Lucy said hello, but already Jesse was hurrying them toward the cemetery, keeping to the shadows to avoid being seen.

"I don't know what kind of ghost goes about with all this furnace and moonlight," Sadie said. "Don't ghosts like the dark better, Joe?"

Joseph grinned and moaned a little. "I reckon they like any night as long as there's someone out there to scare. Boo!"

Lucy, Julia, and Betsy jumped. Joseph laughed.

"Come on," Jesse said. "It'll be darker at the cemetery, and if we're not there by midnight, we might miss him."

Betsy put her hand into Julia's. "We're ready to meet him. Right, Julia?"

Julia nodded. "I want to be able to say I seen him."

"I ain't gonna tell my folks, even if I do see that Tory," said Sadie. "I wouldn't want the whipping for sneaking out."

"It'd be worth the whipping," Julia said, "just to say you were one of the few to see him."

"Ain't nobody gonna see that ghost if we aren't quiet, and if we don't hurry," Jesse said. He motioned them all toward the road to the cemetery.

Lucy walked behind him, hoping that if there was a ghost, she wouldn't be the first to encounter it. As they went farther up the road, the dark enveloped them as the light from the furnace dimmed.

Suddenly a figure stepped out of the dark onto the road. Julia let out a shriek, and Lucy grabbed Jesse's shirt. But when the moon came out from behind the clouds, they could see it was only Jenny Sims. Jenny giggled.

"Aw, what's she doing here?" Jesse complained.

Joseph gave him the evil eye and went on past him to put his arm around his fiancée. "She wants to see the Tory too, don't you, Jen?" Joseph asked, putting his head toward Jenny's.

"All right, then, but stay quiet. No giggling," Jesse said, looking sternly at Jenny.

They continued their procession along the road, passing cow pastures and wagons eerily lit up in the flitting moonlight. The houses began to thin as they approached the bend toward the cemetery. Lucy's heart began to beat faster. Her palms were sweaty. She wiped them down the sides of her dress.

"He's supposed to have been hanged beyond the cemetery, from the oak tree on the other side," Jesse whispered to them all. "Follow me. We'll walk right on through."

Headstones rose from the ground in front of them. The names on each one shone in the threads of moonlight, and the group picked their way among them. Here was old Jonathan Sherwood's grave. He'd died sitting in his rocker last spring. Next was baby Hannah Thorpe's grave, dead at four months from pneumonia. That grave made Lucy sad. Mrs. Thorpe had never really recovered from Hannah's death. It had taken a long time for her to have that child, and so far there had been no more children coming.

Behind her someone coughed, and Lucy jumped. Jesse laughed softly.

"It just startled me," she hissed at him.

"Sure," he said.

Mary Clinton's grave was next. Lucy hated going near that grave. Mary had taken her own life at sixteen, shooting herself one day after hearing that Samuel Bishop, Julia's cousin, was to marry another. Lucy thought she was crazy. Samuel Bishop was an idiot and ugly to boot, but it still gave Lucy the shivers when she thought about Mary standing there, putting a gun to her head, and pulling the trigger.

They neared the tree from which the Tory had been hanged, after he'd tried unsuccessfully to escape a mob of angry colonists. The story went that he had fled to the mountain and been pursued, only to lose his life up here.

The group approached cautiously, walking slowly

in the dark. The night closed in around them. Crickets chirped in the grass at their feet. The wind blew easily. The moon peeped through, then it slipped behind a cloud again, engulfing them in graveyard blackness.

It was during this dark moment that Julia Bishop spoke loudly.

"He ain't here," she said disgustedly. "He ain't coming. I reckon old Ezekiel Johanson saw his shadow that night."

Lucy was inclined to agree. Besides, if everyone agreed, they could go on home, and Lucy was very much in favor of that.

Then she turned and saw a figure rising from behind a tombstone. Lucy's heart froze, and she gasped.

"What is it?" Jesse asked.

Then he saw the figure too. "It's the Tory," he whispered.

The figure stood for a moment in the darkness, then started to move toward them.

"It's him," Julia Sherwood whispered, her voice shaking. "Oh, it's the ghost."

"Hello there." The figure spoke.

Julia and Betsy screamed. Jenny Sims fainted dead away. Joseph, standing stock still, let her drop.

The figure moved with purpose now, and Julia and Betsy fled. Around the tombstones and toward the road, they ran, skirting the figure who was coming closer.

Lucy put her hand in Jesse's. "Let's run," she whispered.

Then the moon came out from behind a cloud, and the graveyard was soaked in light. The figure was revealed. And although he was not from the mountain, it was clear he was not a ghost, either.

Lucy dropped Jesse's hand.

Jesse spoke, but his voice croaked. "Who are you?"

The man came up to them. "Samuel Lernley," he said.

He looked down at the inert Jenny Sims. "Something wrong with her?" he asked.

Joseph gaped, fell to his knees, and began to revive his sweetheart.

"What are you doing in our cemetery?" Jesse asked, his voice stronger now.

"I might ask you the same," Samuel said.

"We live here," Jesse said.

Jenny Sims had come to her senses, and Joseph helped her up.

"I reckon I'd best get her home," Joseph said as he led Jenny, who was no longer giggling, away.

"Perhaps it would be better if you all went home," Samuel suggested. "I don't think your parents would look too kindly on you children being out this late at night."

"Children?" Jesse huffed. "I ain't that much younger than you. So if you think we should be home, I reckon you should be too."

"I'd sure like to be," Samuel said, running a hand through his hair. "But I've got this problem with sleeping. I can't do it easily, so when I wake up, I usually take myself for a walk. That's what I was doing tonight when I decided to sit and rest for a minute against one of these headstones. Never dreamed of being disturbed."

"You're the one disturbing, if I might say so," Jesse said. He eyed Samuel suspiciously. "Were you out here two nights ago?"

Samuel nodded. "I just arrived two evenings past, though I don't see that it's any of your business."

Lucy sighed with relief. "There was no ghost, then. It was just him."

"Ghost?" Samuel said.

"Mr. Johanson come out the night before last and saw a figure in the graveyard," Jesse said. "He thought it was this old Tory ghost that was hanged up here years back."

Samuel laughed. "Sorry to disappoint everybody."

Jesse scowled. "What are you doing here, anyway? You ain't from here."

"I'm from Boston," Samuel said. "I'm staying at Mrs. Brazee's, but I am going to be working for Mr. Jonathan Pettee at his store."

"Mr. Jonathan Pettee?" Jesse said, raising one eyebrow.

Lucy stared at the man. He was to help at the store? Lucy hadn't known her father needed anyone. And there were plenty of people to work for him right here on the mountain.

"Didn't know Mr. Pettee needed another clerk," Jesse said, giving voice to Lucy's question.

"Oh, it's not just for that that I'm here," said Samuel. "I've come to meet his daughter. I guess you could say this is a courting call. Now I've told you who I am. Seems only fair you do the same."

Jesse grinned from ear to ear. "Oh, I'd be glad to, Mr. Lernley. I am Jesse Rosseter and this here," he said, jerking a finger toward Lucy, who was by now somewhere between embarrassed and angry, "is the girl you're to be calling on. Samuel Lernley, meet Lucy Pettee."

9.

Lucy's throat tightened as she stared at the young man in front of her. He had come to court her? Lucy had turned fifteen a few weeks ago, but she still didn't think her father would start being *serious* about this marriage business.

Lucy's mouth suddenly felt dry. She stared at Jesse, who was laughing at the joke, and then at Samuel, who was looking her over. She couldn't stand it. She had to get away. Lucy turned and ran.

Behind her, Jesse yelled for her to stop, but she didn't. She lifted her skirts and fled from the cemetery.

Jesse caught up to her just as she reached the bend in the road that headed toward the furnace. He grabbed her arm, stopping her. Below them, the men were shouting as they did their work, a job that continued twenty-four hours a day.

"You keep running in that direction," Jesse yelled to her above the noise of the furnace, "you'll run right into a bunch of workers. And when they see you, they ain't gonna hold their tongues about you being out alone this late at night, Lucy."

Jesse was right.

"Leave me alone," she said, jerking her arm from his grasp. She had hated meeting Samuel Lernley in the graveyard, but she hated Jesse even more for the way he had laughed. Didn't he know how much it pained her to have him take her marrying someone so lightly?

"I ain't gonna let you take another whipping 'cause of me," Jesse argued with her. He took her by the arm again, nodding his head to indicate that he wished her to walk with him back up the hill, away from the furnace. She followed him in sullen silence.

When they came to a clearing and the noise of the furnace and forges was not so deafening, Jesse stopped.

"I'm sorry, Lucy," he said. "I don't mean to laugh or nothing. It just seems so odd, us being out there with your new suitor in a graveyard at midnight."

"He is NOT my suitor," Lucy protested.

"He thinks he is," Jesse said. He smiled slightly. "Unless tonight has changed his mind."

"It's not funny," Lucy said, fuming.

Jesse nodded. "No," he said. "I reckon it's not."

Lucy went and flopped down on an old fallen log. She covered her face with her hands.

"What am I to do?" Lucy said angrily. "I don't want to leave here. I don't want to go to Boston. I don't want to marry someone I don't even know."

"That won't happen, Luce," Jesse said. "Your father ain't never gonna make you marry someone you don't love. And even if he did, *I* wouldn't let you. So stop worrying about it."

"But he will keep on searching until he finds someone from Boston that I like," Lucy said. "I'll have to leave the mountain eventually."

"Remember what you told me the first day I worked at the pits—that maybe it would be a better life, Lucy?" Jesse reminded her. "Maybe you'd be happier off the mountain."

"How can you say that?" Lucy asked irritably.

"Because I would be. I'd be so happy out at sea

with a boat beneath my legs." Then Jesse said suddenly, "That's it. You should come with me, Lucy. We'll run away together."

Lucy's stomach flipped at the thought of running away with Jesse. But she knew deep down that was an impossible dream.

"Don't be ridiculous, Jesse," she said. "They'd never take a girl in the navy." She kicked at the dirt under her foot. "Everything is all wrong. You have to stay when all you want is to leave, and I have to leave when all I want is to stay."

"Do you want to get married someday, Lucy?" Jesse asked quizzically, as if thinking about the idea for the very first time.

"I don't know," she said slowly, giving it some thought too. "I guess maybe I do. But if it means leaving here, then I'd rather be like old Grandma Brazee with the chickens for company."

Jesse smiled. "Come here, Luce," he said.

He pulled her close, putting his arm around her. She let her head fall on his shoulder, enjoying his warmth. She remembered a few years ago, when they had been about ten and they had fallen asleep while fishing at the lower lake. Lucy had wakened to find herself curled around Jesse's body. It had felt so right, so safe, that Lucy had simply pulled herself closer to him and gone back to sleep. They had both taken a whipping for that.

Now Lucy wished they were back in that sunny day, and that she could again wrap herself around Jesse.

"You ain't gonna marry Samuel Lernley," Jesse whispered softly. "You just can't."

"Why?" Lucy whispered back, wanting him to be right.

"'Cause this mountain wouldn't be the same with you gone, Lucy Pettee," he said.

Lucy looked up into Jesse's eyes, and he gazed back. She leaned toward him, wondering for a moment what it would be like to kiss him. Jesse leaned forward too, his mouth coming toward hers. Lucy felt his breath on her face.

Then Jesse pulled back.

He stood and held out his hand to her.

"It's getting late," he said, his voice cracking. "We'd best be sneaking back in."

He pulled her up. His hand was shaking.

They made their way back toward Lucy's house, and Lucy climbed up the trellis. When she reached her windowsill, she swung her legs over and peered back down into the furnace-lit yard. Jesse stood below, staying to make sure she got safely inside.

"I'm in," Lucy called to him.

He smiled. "Sleep well, Luce, and don't worry," he said firmly. "We'll find a way to rid ourselves of this Samuel Lernley, or my name ain't Jesse Rosseter."

Lucy nodded her head, but there was a lump in her throat. Jesse ran back out into the night, eventually disappearing into the shadows as he made his way down the road toward his own house.

If Jesse hadn't so abruptly turned away earlier, would they have kissed? Lucy almost wished it had happened so she could know what it was like to have his lips on hers. As much as she wanted the relationship between them to stay the same, when she was with him now, Jesse was no longer just plain old Jesse.

And what about Samuel Lernley? Would he come

tomorrow? And if he did, would he hold his tongue when he called? Lucy wondered just what kind of man this Samuel Lernley was.

A knock came to the front door the next morning just as Lucy was dumping a bucket of dirty water, which she had hauled to scrub floors, into the sink.

"Now, who could that be this early?" her father asked.

Lucy put down the wooden bucket.

Her father went out to the front door, and she heard his hello and then a muffled reply. He came back into the kitchen, followed by Samuel.

"Lucy," her father said, clearing his throat, "I'd like you to meet the son of an old friend of mine. Samuel, this is my daughter, Lucy. Lucy, this is Samuel Lernley."

Lucy dried her hands on a dish towel and nodded to Samuel. In the light of morning, she saw that he was about twenty, tall and thin with dark eyes, long lashes, and fair skin that was almost translucent. *Most women would find him handsome,* she thought.

She waited to see if he would say something about already having had the pleasure of meeting her. But he said nothing, simply nodded his greeting.

"Pleased to meet you, Miss Pettee. I'm afraid I may look a bit worn today as I have had trouble sleeping up here. There's a lot of activity at all hours of the night on this mountain," he said, showing an easy smile.

Lucy glared at him. Her father would think he was talking about the blast furnace, but Lucy knew better. It seemed he wasn't going to give her away, but he was certainly going to enjoy teasing her.

"Samuel's here to learn about the business," her father said, his voice gruff. He pulled out a wooden chair and sat down. "He intends to open a store himself, and his parents knew about the quality of goods here on the mountain. I offered to have him learn from me."

"He's not staying here, is he?" Lucy asked.

"No," her father replied, "I didn't think that would be seemly."

"No," Lucy agreed, "it wouldn't be."

"So he's staying with Grandma Brazee," her father said.

"How lovely," Lucy said, smiling widely now at Samuel. She hadn't thought about it last night, but a few more days with old Grandma and Samuel Lernley would probably take to the hills fast. It was really perfect. "I'm sure you'll be happy there."

"Already am," Samuel said, and then, as if he could read her mind, he looked right at her and added, "I'm enjoying myself immensely with Mrs. Brazee."

"Well, Samuel," her father said, "why don't you start on down toward the store? I'll catch up with you directly."

"Yes, sir," Samuel said. "Nice to meet you this morning, Miss Pettee."

She knew he was teasing her again. "Nice to meet you, too, Mr. Lernley."

He walked out of the kitchen to the front hall, and Lucy heard the front door open and close. She turned to look hard at her father, whom she was not about to let win this battle.

"Seems like a nice lad," her father said casually, his eyes wide and innocent.

"Seems so," was all Lucy said.

10.

After her father had left to go to the store, Lucy put on her cap, grabbed a bucket, and headed outside to pick berries. The sun was hot, and she pulled at the collar of her dress. Sweat was quickly snaking its way down her back. But the blueberries needed picking for canning, and if she waited for a cooler day, they might be overripe.

She glanced down the road toward the ironworks. Maybe she could find Jesse and signal him to meet her at the end of the day for a swim. The cool water would be worth the trouble of scrounging through the blueberry bushes and tediously picking, and maybe a swim would help bury these odd feelings and thoughts she'd had lately toward Jesse.

She scooted down the road toward the furnace. Two men went flying by her down the road on horse-drawn wagons stacked with charcoal, limestone, and ore.

"What you doing down here, Lucy?" Julia Bishop's father shouted out. "You best get on home. Don't want you getting hurt."

Lucy nodded and silently cursed. She didn't want her father finding out she had gone near the furnace.

Another wagon roared by her. She jumped out of the way, but this time the cart stopped.

"Lucy," came a warning voice.

It was Joseph, sitting high on his wagon. His face was covered with soot.

"What are you doing here?" he asked. "Women ain't allowed near here. You know that."

He signaled to the crew of another full wagon to go on ahead of him.

"You get in trouble last night?" he asked.

Lucy shook her head. "No," she said. "And Mr. Lernley didn't say anything either, when he came this morning to meet Father."

Joseph smiled. "Nice of him."

Lucy scowled. "I guess so. Though he grinned at me enough when Father wasn't looking."

Joseph laughed. "Well," he said, "I'd best be about my work, and you'd best be about yours."

He turned back toward his wagon, then hesitated. "Lucy, I don't mean to talk out of turn, but do you mind my telling you what I told Jess last night when he finally come in?"

Lucy shrugged. "All right."

"I'm not sure what you want out of life, Luce," he began, "but maybe it'd be best if you really sat and thought about it a bit and then worked out how to get it. You and Jesse are growing up now. You ain't children anymore."

"That's a fate worse than death," Lucy grumbled, thinking about how much she hated these new changes.

Joseph smiled. "Nah," he said. "It seems that way at first, but then you get this picture of what you want, and everything just seems to fit. Stop fighting it, Lucy. Enjoy the growing up."

"Are you talking about Jenny Sims?" Lucy asked.

Joseph nodded. "Yeah, I guess I am."

"You really love her, don't you, Joseph," Lucy said, suddenly serious.

Joseph nodded. "I do," he said. "And I can't wait for our life together. You take some time these next few days to think on what you want. As I told Jess, if it's the sea, then plan on how to get to the sea. If it's something else, then plan on that, too. When you got it right, you'll know it."

Lucy wondered what he meant by "something else."

He flicked the reins over his horse's back and began to steer the wagon down the hill toward the blast furnace. "Now get on home, Lucy," he warned. "This ain't no place for children or women. Don't want you getting hurt."

He smiled back at her, and Lucy watched as he drove his wagon away. The sun was lighting up his hair and his face, and in spite of the soot, Lucy thought she had never seen a man as happy as Joseph Rosseter was at that moment.

Lucy hadn't gone very far back up the hill toward home when she heard the whistle from the furnace. The whistle only sounded when there was an accident.

Lucy's heart raced. Could it be Jesse? Although he was away from the furnace and forges, there had been incidents in the past when a collier had been burned.

All around her now, women and children were pouring out of their homes or coming in from their fields, heading down the hill. When there was trouble, everyone ran to the blast furnace, anxious to make sure it was not their loved one who was hurt.

Lucy felt the worry too, yet she stood still, unable to make herself move. She could not bear it if Jesse had been injured.

Soon, though, she was caught up with the crowd as they made their way down the hillside to where the Wachocastinook Creek left the lower lake. She was pushed and shoved all the way there, until the women and children stopped and stood in a group near the furnace. In spite of the apparent accident, work continued, flames shooting out of the vent pipe, the roar of the furnace filling the air. The furnace could not stop suddenly, not for anyone or anything. Once stopped, there would be no iron, no money.

"Who's hurt?" shouted one woman.

“Yes. Who is it?” another called out.

Lucy felt a jostling at her side. Her father had pushed his way toward her with Samuel Lernley right behind him.

Lucy’s father put an arm around her shoulders. His eyes were grave.

Lucy was tapped again, and she turned to find Jesse’s mother beside her.

“Have they said?” she asked, her face drawn with worry.

“Not yet,” Lucy’s father answered. “Here, Maggie. Let me take the little one from you.”

Lucy’s father lifted Polly from Mrs. Rosseter’s arms. Lucy picked up Annie who was clinging to Mrs. Rosseter’s skirts.

There was a sudden shifting in the crowd.

“Here comes someone,” a woman shouted. “Who is it? Who’s hurt?”

Lucy strained but could see no one. Was it Jesse? Was he injured? Why wasn’t he here at the edge of the furnace with everyone else? Most of the other colliers were already standing there in the crowd, grimy with soot. Lucy felt sick to her stomach.

Then the crowd began to part, murmuring as they did, and she breathed a sigh of relief as she saw Jesse walking toward them.

"He's all right," she murmured. Her father squeezed her shoulder.

But Jesse was walking slowly.

A hand gripped hers. Mrs. Rosseter was squeezing tightly, and her face was white.

Jesse approached them.

"It's Joseph, Ma," he said.

11.

Jesse hugged his mother after giving her the bad news. He looked at Lucy but said nothing. Then he led his mother down to the furnace opening to see her son. Lucy heard from the crowd that the doctor was there now. Joseph wasn't dead, but he was badly burned.

"Come on, Lucy," her father said. "There's nothing we can do for the Rosseters here. Why don't we take Annie and Polly back to their house and get some food ready for them? They're going to need it."

Lucy nodded. She wanted to be with Jesse, but she knew her father was speaking the truth. There was nothing she could do for them there. It was best to help out by watching the little ones.

She set Annie down and began to follow her father back up the hill toward the Rosseters' house.

The crowd was breaking up now as other men from the furnace made their way up the hill, finding their wives and children and hugging them tight before heading back to work.

"Can I do something to help?" Samuel asked, coming to Lucy's side.

Lucy had forgotten about him and looked at him in surprise. He gazed at her, uncertain and awkward, and she felt sorry for him. He wasn't from the mountain, and in this crowd of people who knew each other so well, he would truly feel it. Lucy took pity on him.

"I'm sure we could use a hand at the Rosseters'," she said.

Samuel nodded and walked beside her as they made their way up the hill. Annie tugged at Lucy's skirts.

"Joe's hurt, ain't he?" Annie asked. Lucy stopped and knelt down next to her.

Annie's lip began to quiver as Lucy thought about what to say. Should she tell her the truth? Lucy hesitated, then took a deep breath.

"Yes, Annie, Joseph has been hurt," Lucy said. "We don't know how badly yet, so you mustn't worry until we know if there is something to be concerned about. Mr. Pettee, Mr. Lernley, and I are going to take you home now, and we will wait there for your mother to come back and tell us how Joseph is. But I do know one thing, Annie."

"What?" Annie asked, sticking her finger in her mouth.

"Your mother is going to need you. Even if Joseph is just a little hurt, it will take him some time to get better," Lucy said. "Your mother is going to need you to help as she cares for him. Can you do that?"

Annie nodded her head.

Then Lucy stood. Samuel was watching her closely.

"Come on, Lucy," Annie said. "We gotta get home to help Ma."

Lucy looked away from Samuel. "Yes, Annie," she said. "That's just what we should do."

They began to walk up the hill again.

Beside her, Samuel cleared his throat. "Awful hard business, this ironwork," he said sympathetically.

Lucy nodded. "It is hard," she agreed. "Accidents do happen, but bad ones are rare."

Samuel nodded thoughtfully. "Seems a bit noisy and dirty."

"Yes," Lucy said, realizing he had mirrored her own thoughts on the process, "but it's only for a few months. The winter months are peaceful."

"You're not lonely then," Samuel asked, "being up here without much to do?"

Lucy shook her head firmly. "No, Mr. Lernley," she said emphatically, "lonely is the one thing I am not."

Then she marched resolutely ahead, leaving Samuel to follow in her wake.

Lucy's father was already at the Rosseter household when Lucy, Annie, and Samuel arrived. Sadie and Mary looked up when Lucy came into the kitchen. Their eyes were red from crying. The butter churn lay forlornly beside Sadie, while Mary's carding combs sat on the kitchen table, the wool still stuck in their picks.

"Come, come," Lucy's father was saying. "We don't know yet what has happened. This is no time for tears."

"We gotta help Ma," Annie said. "We gotta finish our chores."

"That's right, Annie," Lucy's father said.

"Did you see him, Lucy?" Mary asked, her voice hopeful.

Lucy shook her head. "No, I'm sorry, Mary. I know as little as the rest of you."

"If only Ma had let us go with her when the whistle sounded," Sadie said. "We might be there now, helping Joseph."

"Your mother needs help here, too, Sadie," Lucy's father said.

There was a shuffling noise from the other room. Grandpa came into the kitchen, reaching out to grab something to steady himself. Lucy's father went immediately to the old man and helped him into a chair.

"What's all the commotion about?" Grandpa shouted.

Lucy went and knelt in front of him. "Joseph's been hurt, Grandpa," she yelled so that he could hear.

"Bad off?" Grandpa asked, his brow wrinkled with concern.

"We don't know yet," Lucy said to him. "We're waiting for Mrs. Rosseter to return with news."

From the corner of her eye, Lucy saw that Samuel had drawn water from the kitchen pump and put it in a pot on the stove to boil. He was preparing tea. She stood to go help him.

"Sadie and Mary," Lucy said, "would you mind helping Samuel and me prepare some food?"

"How can we eat with Joseph hurt?" Sadie asked.

"Eating is what you should do, Sadie," Lucy's father said. "You're going to need your strength for your mother's and Joseph's sakes."

Reluctantly, Sadie returned to her churning, and Mary rose to help Samuel and Lucy heat some beans and salted pork to go with the bread her mother had made earlier. Lucy's father sat with Grandpa at the table, bouncing Polly on his knee. The room was strangely silent. Even Annie made little noise as she moved about the kitchen, sweeping and doing her part to help her mother.

There was a sudden cry from the other room, which made them all jump.

"It's Daniel," Sadie said, removing her apron and

setting aside her churning. "He was napping in the other room. I'll go get him."

She left, and Lucy turned back to the stove and her pot of beans, glancing out the window as she did. Up the road from the furnace, a procession was approaching, and a figure on a stretcher was being carried toward the house.

"They're coming," she whispered.

"I'll pull down Ma and Pa's bed," Mary said. "They can take him right in there."

"Good idea, Mary," Lucy's father said, rising. "I'll see if they need help outside."

"I'll take the baby, sir," Samuel said, holding out his arms for baby Polly.

Polly fussed at being handed to someone she didn't know, but as Samuel rocked her gently back and forth, she stopped her crying.

"Thank you, Samuel," Lucy's father said.

Her father donned his hat and left the room. From the window, Lucy watched him make his way toward the approaching party.

"Can you see anything, Lucy?" Sadie asked. "Can you tell if my brother is badly hurt?"

Lucy shook her head. "I can't see a thing yet, Sadie."

Samuel was stirring the beans on the stove, Polly on his hip. He looked totally at ease, as if he did this every day. Lucy wondered how and where he had learned to cook. His eyes met hers, but he said nothing.

Lucy turned back to the window. Sadie had come to stand beside her, Daniel in her arms. They were getting close now, and Lucy could make out Jesse. He had a fierce look on his face. Lucy's father had joined them, and he and Mr. Rosseter were shouldering the stretcher. The doctor and Mrs. Rosseter were behind them, moving quickly.

Then they were near the house, and Lucy drew in her breath. She could see Joseph. His face was red with welts all along one side, and his right arm hung from the stretcher, swollen and burnt. Lucy swallowed hard.

She went to the door and opened it to let them all in.

12.

The sight of Joseph up close was even worse than Lucy had expected. His flesh smelled horribly. They bumped the stretcher slightly carrying him inside, and Joseph moaned a little.

"Watch out," Lucy's father shouted. "We need to get him into the back room."

As they made their way through the kitchen, soot from their shoes dropped onto the wooden floorboards. Annie swiftly swept it up.

"Sadie," Mrs. Rosseter said, "run out to the spring-house and bring me some butter. Hurry now."

Jesse came in behind them. He stood in the kitchen, staring after the others. Lucy went to him and put her head on his shoulder.

"I'm sorry," she whispered to him.

He turned unseeing eyes her way and then began

to shake. She put her arms around him and led him to the kitchen table. She made him sit, all the while holding him tightly. She wanted to pour all her love into him, to help give him strength.

"Why?" he breathed softly. "Why Joe?"

Sadie was sobbing when she came back into the kitchen after delivering the butter to her mother. Mary, too, was crying. Lucy reached out a free hand and touched both their cheeks. Grandpa sat at the table with them, staring off into the distance.

Lucy's father came back into the kitchen. His face was grim.

"Oh, Mr. Pettee," Sadie said, jumping up and wiping away her tears. "Is he gonna be all right?"

Lucy's father shook his head. "I'm sorry, honey," he said. "The doctor's with him now, and we have to wait to see what he says."

"Wait, wait, wait," Sadie said, stomping her foot. "That's all we keep on hearing."

"I know, Sadie," Lucy's father said, hugging her to him. "I know."

"How'd it happen?" Grandpa shouted out.

Lucy's father went over to him and took a seat.

"Apparently he was unloading his wagon into the top of the furnace, and he must have not been paying attention. He got too close and some sparks shot up and caught his shirt."

Lucy thought about her earlier conversation with Joseph. Had her words made him more careless? Had talking about Jenny Sims caused him to stop concentrating on a job that needed all the concentration one had? And where was Jenny? Why wasn't she here?

Lucy thought about saying something then decided against it. She didn't want to upset the family more than they already were. Jenny's simpering ways were not what they needed now, anyway.

The kitchen door swung open, and Mrs. Rosseter came into the room.

Lucy's father grabbed a chair and pulled it out for her. "Sit, Maggie," he said.

Mrs. Rosseter sank wearily into the chair.

"How is he, Ma?" Sadie asked quietly.

Mrs. Rosseter raised her head. Her eyes were shining. "We don't know yet, honey. He'll have scars, I reckon. The doctor will be out to talk with us as soon as he can."

“Gotta be careful at that place. All kinds of dangers there,” Grandpa shouted out.

“That damn furnace will eat you alive if you let it,” Jesse said angrily.

“Please, Jesse,” Mrs. Rosseter said softly. “Not now.”

“Can I get you a cup of tea?” Lucy asked.

Mrs. Rosseter nodded. “That would be fine, Lucy.”

Her eyes swept around the room. “Where are Polly and Daniel and Annie?” she asked, her voice rising with concern.

Now that Lucy thought about it, she hadn’t seen Jesse’s youngest siblings since Joseph had been brought in. And Samuel seemed to be missing, too.

“That fellow from down off took the young’uns outside somewhere,” Grandpa shouted. “Good of him too. Ain’t a pretty sight for those little ones to see.”

Lucy nodded, glad that Samuel had done this. She wished that she had thought of it herself. Seeing Joseph burnt like that just might have given Annie nightmares, something Mrs. Rosseter didn’t need now.

"What fellow from down off?" Mrs. Rosseter asked.

Lucy brought over some tea.

"His name's Samuel Lernley," Lucy's father said. "No need to worry, Maggie. He's helping me out at the shop. They'll be all right with him."

Mrs. Rosseter nodded and took a drink. A loud moan came from the back room, followed by a scream of pain. Mrs. Rosseter abruptly set the cup down. Tears came to her eyes.

"Maggie?" Lucy's father said, stepping closer.

Mrs. Rosseter waved him away. "No, I'm all right, Jonathan. Thank you."

"Was that Joseph, Ma?" Mary asked, her voice shaking.

"Come here, Mary," Mrs. Rosseter said.

Mary went and sat on her mother's lap. At eight, she was unwieldy, all arms and legs, but her mother didn't seem to mind.

"Joseph is gonna be in a lot of pain the next few weeks," Mrs. Rosseter said quietly. "I don't want this to scare you, but he's gonna need our understanding. All right?"

Mary nodded. She buried her head in her mother's shoulder.

The doctor came into the room, followed by Mr. Rosseter, who went to the sink to wash his hands. Mrs. Rosseter started to get up, but the doctor nodded for her to sit.

"He's asleep, Maggie," the doctor said. "So relax now, and have your tea. You'll be busy enough with him when he wakes."

"Is he gonna be all right?" Mrs. Rosseter asked, her voice barely a whisper.

The doctor sighed and set his bag down on the table. "He'll live, if that's what you're asking. But I'm not going to give you any pretty story. He's going to have bad scars. His face won't be the same. As for the arm, only time will tell. I'm hoping he'll get use of it back, but I can't be sure yet. We'll just have to wait and see on that. For now, I suggest you make an herbal brew for him. He'll be in a lot of pain."

Mrs. Rosseter turned her face away, biting her lip.

"Damn that furnace," Jesse muttered. "Grandpa's hearing almost gone 'cause of it, and Joseph burned."

"I ain't gonna have you talking like that," Mr.

Rosseter roared, swinging around from the sink at Jesse's words. "That furnace and these forges have provided this family a decent living. It's a good life working here on this mountain, and I ain't gonna have you saying otherwise."

"I'll say what I see," Jesse shouted back, standing and knocking over his chair in the process. "And I see a lot of hurt in this family from these ironworks."

"Maybe you should look a little closer then, boy," Mr. Rosseter yelled. "You got a lot of mighty fine things here too."

"Things?" Jesse yelled. "You reckon these things are more important than Joseph's face or the use of his arm?"

"Did I say that?" Mr. Rosseter yelled back.

Mrs. Rosseter rose. "Enough!" Her voice was steely cold.

"Enough," she repeated when Jesse and Mr. Rosseter had grown silent. "My son is hurt, and I ain't gonna have you bickering in this household until he is better, you hear me?"

Both Jesse and Mr. Rosseter nodded.

The doctor cleared his throat and picked up his

bag and hat. "I'm going on home, Maggie," he said. "I'll be back later to check in on him."

Mrs. Rosseter nodded and showed him to the door.

Lucy rose too. "I think we could all do with something to eat," she said.

"I'll help," her father said.

Lucy went to the stove. Beside her, Mr. Rosseter stood, his head bent over the sink. She glanced over at him and saw the stern man's face was twisted with anguish.

Lucy wanted to reach out and comfort him, but she didn't know how. And she didn't know if he would want that. So she took a deep breath and said as easily as she could, "We could use some more firewood, Mr. Rosseter. Do you think you could fetch me some?"

Mr. Rosseter reached up and quickly wiped his eyes. He cleared his throat. "I'll be glad to get some, Lucy. We appreciate you taking the time to help us here."

Then without another word, he went outside. Jesse glared after him. And Lucy wished that it had been Jesse, not her, who had seen this proud man breaking down.

Lucy and her father walked home slowly that night. They said little. Lucy felt as if she would fall asleep right there in the road if she stopped for only a minute. When they neared their house, they saw lights on inside.

"Now what?" Lucy's father said.

As they drew closer, a figure came down the steps from the dark of thc porch. It was Samuel Lernley with Polly in his arms.

"I hope you don't mind, sir," he said, "but I brought the Rosseter children here for tonight. I figured that family didn't need the little ones hanging on them, wanting things, and I didn't know where else to take them. Mrs. Brazee seemed a little put out with the children at her house. I figured you were closer to the family than maybc shc is, anyway."

Annie and Daniel were on the porch.

"Thank you, Samuel," Lucy's father said, taking Polly from him. "You did the right thing. I'm sorry I didn't think of it myself."

Samuel nodded. "Well, now that you're here, I'll be heading down to Mrs. Brazee's."

Samuel had quietly and efficiently taken care of so much today. Lucy hesitated, but only for a minute. "Would you like a bite to eat before you go, Mr. Lernley?" she asked.

Samuel smiled. "No thank you, Miss Pettee," he said. "Mrs. Brazee fed me along with the children. She sent a little something up for you, too."

"Thank you, Samuel," Lucy's father said.

"Yes, thank you, Mr. Lernley," Lucy said, feeling a smile peep out, though it seemed wrong with everything that had happened. "And thank Grandma, too."

"Good night, then," Samuel said. He walked away from them.

Lucy followed her father and the children into the house. She could smell the food still warm on the stove. She looked thoughtfully back through the screen door at Samuel.

"Funny how Mr. Lernley seemed so capable of handling children and cooking," Lucy said to her father.

Her father stood beside her for a moment, rocking Polly. "It's not all that hard to understand, Luce," he said. "Samuel's sister died in childbirth, and her husband took off, leaving the kids for Samuel's parents to raise. They're on the older side, and as I understand it from them, Samuel pretty much raised those kids himself so his parents weren't so burdened. Awful decent of him, don't you think?"

Lucy nodded, his words giving her pause.

"I'm going to go change out of these grimy clothes, and then I'll be down," she said softly.

Lucy went to her room and leaned out her window for a moment. In the light from the furnace, she could just make out the retreating figure of Samuel walking down the road toward Grandma Brazee's. As she watched the man go, an odd feeling stirred inside her that she would have been hard-pressed to describe. But if she had been made to, Lucy Pettee would have said that it made her feel queer to watch Samuel Lernley's tall, lean form walking in the shadows, as if goose bumps were covering her flesh. To her surprise, it wasn't an unpleasant feeling.

13.

Lucy woke to the bright sunshine of a warm and glorious summer morning. She rolled over lazily in bed, drawing the quilt up higher over her head to shut out the noise of the furnace. Then the events of the day before came back to her. She sat up, her only thought now was of how Joseph had survived the night.

She spied a set of eyes peering at her over the foot of her brass bed. Lucy smiled, and instantly, Annie was up on Lucy's bed, snuggling in next to her with a thumb in her mouth.

"And how did you sleep, little one?" Lucy asked, taking in Annie's child smell and feeling her spirits lift just to have Annie's tiny body so close.

"Daniel kicked me," Annie said crossly. "I don't like sleeping with him."

Lucy smiled. "And is your brother awake now?"

Annie nodded. "I told him to stay still while I went to find you."

Lucy nodded. "Good thinking, Annie. I'd better get up and get some breakfast for you and Daniel."

"Luce?" Annie said, tugging on Lucy's nightgown. "How come we stayed here with you? Can we do it again? And is Joseph hurt bad?"

Lucy sighed and gathered Annie up again in her arms. "Yes, Annie. Joseph is hurt bad. You may have to stay with us for a while."

"I like staying with you, Lucy," Annie said. "But I reckon it would be best if I slept with you and not with Daniel."

"Oh, really?" Lucy said, smiling again. "We'll see."

A patter of little feet on the floorboards was heard outside Lucy's room. Daniel poked his head around the door.

"Daniel hungry," he said, a frown on his face.

"You're always hungry," Annie said. "And I told you to stay in bed."

"Hungry," Daniel said again.

Lucy nodded. "All right, all right. Breakfast it is."

She rose from bed just as Polly began to fuss from Lucy's old trundle bed in the other room. Lucy shook her head, wondering how Mrs. Rosseter kept up with this busy crowd day in and day out.

Lucy frowned at the burnt corn mush in the pot. Jesse was right. She wasn't much of a cook. There was a knock at the back door. Lucy put the pot down and went to open it.

"Samuel," Annie shouted. She ran to him and gave him a big hug.

"I hope I'm not intruding," Samuel said as he picked up Annie. "How'd you children sleep?"

"Daniel kicked me all night," Annie said, frowning.

"My sister used to kick me in bed too," Samuel said.

"What'd you do?" Annie asked.

"Kicked her back," Samuel said, winking. "But not so hard that she'd squeal on me to Mama."

Annie giggled.

Daniel tottered over to Samuel and offered him a piece of chewed-up bread.

"Thank you kindly, Daniel," Samuel said, bending down to take the soggy piece.

Lucy laughed. She couldn't help it.

Samuel looked up and caught her eye.

"We truly appreciate all the help you've given, Mr. Lernley," Lucy said, blushing.

"No trouble," Samuel said. He gave a rueful smile. "To tell the truth I've got a niece and two nephews back in Boston. I miss them something terrible when I'm gone from them, and taking care of these kids was a bit of a salve."

"My father told me last night you were responsible for raising your sister's children," Lucy said. "That's very commendable, Mr. Lernley."

"I wouldn't go that far," Samuel said. "My parents are very involved, but I do help out when I can. My sister and I were close, and it's important to me that her children are well taken care of."

"Won't your parents need some help now that you're here?" Lucy asked.

Samuel laughed. "I'm sure they will. Those kids are a handful. But I don't plan on staying more than a month or two. My father and I are in the process of buying a store in Boston. He knew your father would be the man to train me, and, too, my parents didn't want me to ignore my own life. I want a wife and children some day, and they don't want the responsibility of taking care of my sister's children to overshadow my own desires."

Lucy felt that strange feeling deep in her gut again. She looked away, her thoughts spinning about uncomfortably.

Samuel cleared his throat. "I didn't know what your father had in mind today about the store, in light of the accident . . . ," he said. His voice trailed off.

Lucy's father came down the stairs. "Who's here, Lucy?" he called.

"Mr. Lernley, Father," Lucy called back.

"Hello, Samuel," Mr. Pettee said, coming into the kitchen. "Do you think you could open the shop with Eric today? Lucy's going to run some food down to the Rosseters. I don't think making breakfast will be much on their minds this morning. And I will have to keep an eye on these little ones."

"Yes, sir," Samuel said. "I think we can manage."

"Good," her father said. "Go on, then, Lucy."

Lucy hurriedly dished some of the corn mush she'd made into another bowl, trying to avoid the burnt parts. Samuel opened the door for her, and Lucy ducked under his arm with her breakfast for the Rosseters, glad to escape Samuel and further discussion of his future plans.

As she started down the road, she looked back. Samuel was still standing at the kitchen door, watching her walk away.

Lucy knocked lightly on the Rosseters' door, and Sadie opened it, holding a finger to her lips.

"Sssh," she said. "Joseph's finally sleeping."

"Bad night?" Lucy asked.

"Awful," Sadie said. "He was screaming something terrible, Luce. Made me want to cover my ears and run away. Ma's exhausted."

On the table were dozens of covered plates. Lucy looked down at her own measly corn mush.

"Guess you don't need breakfast," she said.

Sadie shook her head. "People have been bringing food all morning," she said, "but none of us feels like eating."

Lucy came into the house and set her corn mush down on the stove. "Where's Jesse?" she asked.

"At the charcoal pits," Sadie said quietly.

Lucy's heart stopped. "What?" she whispered.

"Pa made him go," Sadie said. "Pa went too. Said they had a job to do."

"Poor Jess," Lucy said, knowing how much Jesse had probably wanted to stay by his brother's side. Of all the days to send Jesse to the charcoal pits, this must have been the worst.

"Actually, Lucy," Sadie said, "I'm awful glad you're here. Mary and I have been trying to help Grandpa get dressed. His fingers can't work all the buttons on his shirt and breeches, but I don't want to bother Ma. Do you mind giving us a hand?"

"Of course not," Lucy said.

She followed Sadie down the hall toward Grandpa's room. They passed Mr. and Mrs. Rosseter's room, where Joseph lay, still and quiet. Mrs. Rosseter looked up from Joseph's bedside when Lucy passed. She smiled slightly, but her eyes were rimmed with dark circles.

Back in Grandpa's room, the three girls steadied

Grandpa while he pulled on his breeches and shirt. They buttoned him up. For once, Grandpa did not shout out his thoughts, and Lucy was glad. His voice might have wakened Joseph, and Joe needed all the rest his burnt body would give him.

Together they helped Grandpa shuffle down the hall. He stopped briefly by the door to Mr. and Mrs. Rosseter's room and looked in at Joseph but said nothing. When they finally got him seated at the table, he didn't touch his breakfast.

There was a knock at the back door, and Lucy opened it to find a very serious Jenny Sims on the step.

Her eyes were lowered. "I come to see Joe," she said.

Lucy nodded and let Jenny in. Sadie turned her head away and muttered, "'Bout time."

"I'm scared," Jenny said softly. "Some say he won't heal. He'll be scarred and maybe lose his arm. That right?"

"Yeah, maybe," Sadie snapped. "And we're all scared, Jenny, including Joseph."

Lucy raised her hand. "Sssh, Sadie," she said. "I think Jenny's doing the best she can."

Sadie snorted and went outside.

Mary, too, turned away.

"Can I see him?" Jenny asked, her voice small.

Lucy nodded. "He's sleeping."

"I'll be quiet," Jenny said.

Lucy led Jenny down the hall toward the Rosseters' bedroom. As they approached, she heard Mrs. Rosseter talking softly. Joseph was awake.

"Mrs. Rosseter," Lucy said, "Jenny Sims is here to see Joseph."

"Bring her on in, Lucy," Mrs. Rosseter said.

Lucy nodded her head toward the room. Jenny approached the doorway. She stared for a moment at Joseph on the bed, then she let out a little moan. Without another word, she brushed past Lucy and ran back down the hallway toward the kitchen. Lucy followed her, calling her name softly, but Jenny did not stop. She ran outside, past a startled Sadie, who was feeding the chickens in the yard. Lucy called out more loudly now, chasing Jenny halfway up the hill before finally, Jenny stopped. Her shoulders were heaving, and she was sobbing.

"Jenny," Lucy said severely, panting from the run,

shouting to be heard above the noise of the furnace. "You can't just run out on Joseph like that. He's ill, and he needs your support. What were you thinking?"

Jenny shook her head. "He looks bad," she said between cries. "I don't even recognize his face."

Lucy stared at the distraught girl. "Of course he looks terrible, but he'll heal. You'll marry, and things will be fine. Right now Joseph needs you, Jenny."

Jenny shook her head over and over. "I can't," she said. "I can't go in there with him looking like that. You don't understand.

"There ain't no Joseph and me anymore, Lucy," Jenny shouted. "I can't live with him all burnt like that. I come to tell him, but I can't. You gotta do it."

Then without another word, Jenny lifted her skirts and ran farther up the hill toward her home.

"Jenny!" Lucy screamed as the horror of what Jenny had left her to do sunk in. "You coward! You come back here right now!"

"JENNY!" Lucy screamed, panic engulfing her. "JENNY!"

"What are you screaming so loud at Jenny Sims for this early in the morning?" came a sour voice.

Jesse was standing behind her, staring at Jenny running up the hill.

"I . . . ," Lucy began, then she paused. She wasn't sure if she should tell Jesse why she was yelling. What if Jesse took off after Jenny? He might kill her, the way he was feeling.

"You what?" Jesse said grumpily.

Lucy paused. "She ran out on your brother, said she couldn't stay with him." Lucy didn't say it was for good.

Jesse scowled. "Better off without her, anyway," he said. "All her silly giggling would stop him from resting. I don't see why you're so hot to bring her back. I say let her go."

He moved off the road a bit, pulling Lucy with him. A horse went by carrying saddlebags filled with ore that creaked and groaned as they swayed back and forth.

Lucy watched the horse make its way toward the hill behind the furnace. If only Jesse knew that Jenny would not be coming back at all. Lucy took a deep breath and steadied her voice. "I guess you're right." She paused. "What are you doing here? Why aren't you at the pits?"

Jesse shook his head derisively. "They done give me the day off," he said. "As a kind of celebration, I guess."

"Celebration?" Lucy said, shocked. "For what?"

Jesse scowled. "Well," he said, his voice heavy with sarcasm, "since Joseph got injured, they wanted to thank our family for their service to the ironworks. So the forge master come to see me this morning. He's gonna move me up and give me Joe's old job. Starting tomorrow I get to work the furnace. Now, ain't that lucky?"

14.

"You're teasing me, Jesse Rosseter, aren't you?" Jesse at the furnace? Jesse working the same job that had burnt Joseph so badly? Not her Jesse!

Jesse shook his head. "Nah, Luce. I wish I was."

He bent down, picked up a stone from the road, and sent it flying. "Pa even come over to tell me that he was glad," Jesse said. "Said he knew I would work hard and do him proud."

Jesse paused. "Had to remind him just why I got moved up in the first place, and he stomped off."

"He should have thought about it before he said that," Lucy said softly.

"I reckon he should've, but you and I know he usually don't." Jesse sighed. "So anyway," he went on, "for better or worse I'm to work at the furnace starting tomorrow. And seeing as I'd like to forget that piece of news, I was wondering how heavy your chores are today?"

Lucy knew she had a lot to do. They were low on candles, and she should bake some bread. But she couldn't let Jesse down.

"Not heavy enough I can't put them aside for a while," Lucy said. "Your brother and sisters are up at my house. You want to take them to the Old Landing?"

Jesse nodded. "I would. But let me go check on Ma and Joseph first. See if they need anything. I'll meet you back at your place."

Lucy nodded and watched him run down the hill toward his house. With a weary step, she started toward home.

Screams of delight came from her house. Lucy was surprised to look through the screen door and find Samuel Lernley down on all fours giving Daniel and Annie, both in their nightclothes, a ride in the hall.

Lucy wondered what he was still doing there when he was supposed to be at the store. She watched them unseen, a smile coming to her lips. He really was very good with children.

Samuel loped toward the front door.

"Faster, Samuel, faster," Annie cried.

Samuel picked up speed, crawling as fast as he could on his hands and knees. He reached the front screen door and looked up. His face turned red.

"Lucy!" Annie cried, sliding from Samuel's back. "Samuel's playing horse with us. I've named him Whinny."

"Whinny?" Lucy said, as she opened the screen door and stepped inside.

Samuel slid Daniel off his back and rose sheepishly to his knees.

"More, more," Daniel said, tugging on Samuel's leg.

"Sorry, son," Samuel said. "Miss Pettee's here now to take you. I've got to be getting back to the store."

"Whinny has other chores to do today," Lucy said, laughing.

Samuel looked down at the floor, then he laughed too.

"Where's my father?" Lucy asked.

"Upstairs," Samuel replied. "He said he'd be down

shortly. Eric Moseman sent me up to get him. Something needs your father's attention at the store."

"Why does Samuel gotta go? Why?" Annie cried.

Lucy saw their disappointment over Samuel leaving.

"Annie," Lucy said, "take your brother upstairs and put on some clothes. I'm going to take you for a swim at a very special place today."

Annie's eyes lit up. "Come on, Daniel," she said. "We're going swimming."

Annie led Daniel away, tugging impatiently at her brother, who was toddling as fast as he could behind her.

Samuel smiled. "That'd be a nice way to spend the day with them, Miss Pettee. Annie's been asking to go see her brother, but a swim might take her mind off him for a while."

At the mention of Joseph, Lucy remembered Jenny Sims and what she would eventually have to tell Joseph.

"Something wrong, Miss Pettee?" Samuel asked.

Lucy shook her head quickly. "No, nothing's wrong, Mr. Lernley," she said.

Samuel looked at her more closely, as if he didn't believe her, and Lucy blushed. She pushed open the porch door and stepped back outside.

He followed her. "You sure nothing's wrong, Miss Pettee?"

"I . . . ," she began, then stopped. What was she thinking? She was about to blurt out Jenny's story, to a stranger no less!

Samuel put a hand on her arm. "Something is bothering you, Miss Pettee," he said. "You can tell me what it is. I promise I won't tell a soul."

Samuel was watching her, waiting patiently. An incredible urge to unburden herself to him surged through her. She knew he could keep a secret. He had done it before.

"Lucy!" Annie yelled out from just inside the screen door. "Why does Samuel have his hand on your arm?"

Lucy pulled back, suddenly aware of Samuel touching her.

"I'd like to know the same thing," came a voice from the side of the house. It was Jesse.

Lucy wanted to sink into the ground.

"Jesse!" Annie cried, running out onto the porch

and down the steps toward her brother. "Are you coming swimming with us?"

Samuel stepped away from Lucy. He threw a glance at Jesse, and his eyes darkened. "I think I'll head on down to the store. Please tell your father where I've gone."

Lucy nodded. She couldn't look him in the face. What had prompted her to almost open herself up to him, to let him put his arm on her like that?

Samuel walked away, nodding curtly at Jesse as he passed him on the hill.

Jesse came and stood by Lucy. "Ain't gonna get rid of him if you keep on letting him touch you," he said angrily.

"I haven't been *letting* him touch me," Lucy huffed. "I just . . . I just . . . oh, I don't know how it happened." She stomped her foot, angry at herself, angry at Samuel Lernley, and angry at Jesse now too.

"Makes me wonder if you still want to get rid of him, Luce," Jesse said.

"Of course I want to get rid of him," Lucy asserted. "I told you so, didn't I?"

"What people say and what people do ain't

always the same thing," Jesse said gruffly.

"Sometimes I hate you, Jesse," Lucy said through her teeth. "I truly and thoroughly hate you."

Jesse looked at her. "You know what they say, Luce. Hate is the closest thing to love."

Lucy stared at him.

Then Jesse smiled slowly. "Oh, stop growling at me, Lucy. Let's go have us some fun."

The water in the lake was warm and beautiful. Lucy swam farther and farther out. It seemed, if only for a minute, that as long as she kept on swimming, all her worries about Joseph's accident, about Jenny Sims breaking off their engagement, and about Jesse starting work at the furnace could be cast out into the water and allowed to drift lazily away. She didn't want to stop. But at last she was tired, and when she reached the island in the middle of the lake, she stepped out and climbed up onto the rocks.

Across the water, Jesse was holding baby Polly at the lake's edge. Polly screamed excitedly when her toes touched the water. Her little legs went round and round, splashing Jesse.

Jesse was bent over, the light from the water reflecting on his face. *This is how he would look as a father,* Lucy thought.

Jesse looked out to her and waved. He was happy, and Lucy's stomach fluttered, wishing he could be happy like this always, wishing this was enough for him, wishing that maybe *she* would be enough for him.

Annie was swimming just a bit out from the shore. "Come back, Lucy," she called. "Come back and play with us."

Lucy nodded and waded into the water to begin the swim back. When she got there, she dove beneath the surface, peering into its depths to find Annie's legs. She grabbed one and heard Annie's squeal of delight above the surface.

She stood up. Annie was jumping up and down in the waist-high water.

"Carry me. Carry me," Daniel called out to Lucy from the shore, holding out his arms.

"Thanks a lot, Luce," Jesse said. "You go for a nice long swim, leaving me with all this?"

He grinned at her. Lucy smiled back.

"I'll take them for a while," she said. "You can go on and swim."

"Nah," Jesse said. There was a sadness in his voice. "I reckon I'll just stay here."

Lucy looked questioningly at him, but Jesse said nothing more.

Later the children lay drowsily in the sun, sleeping off the effects of energy spent in the water. Jesse had eventually gone out for a long swim, and when he returned, Lucy met him at the shore.

"What are you up to?" she asked.

"What do you mean?" he asked as she handed him a rag to dry off with.

"Jesse, I know you better than anyone," Lucy said, "and you're up to something."

Jesse sighed. "You ain't gonna like it, Luce."

"Tell me anyway," Lucy said.

"Proving Day's two months away," Jesse said.

"Sure," Lucy said, "I know." Proving Day came once a year in mid-October, when representatives from the navy came to the mountain. It was a day of celebration with dancing, feasting, and many dignitaries.

This year, as always, the men from the ironworks would be dropping several newly made anchors from the top of an iron tripod to "prove" the anchors were strong enough to hold any ship in a storm. Many of the anchors in the navy had been made on the mountain, including the anchor on "Old Ironsides," the USS *Constitution*—the great battleship in the War of 1812. In addition, the navy also purchased other items from the forge, such as nails, kettles, chains, and latches.

It was a grand day when the mountain people were paid for all the hard work of the blast furnace and forges that year. Ladies came out in their finest silks. Men dressed in their best evening wear. Even the people from down off came up to celebrate. The mountain was filled with strangers, but everyone was in a celebratory mood, so even Lucy didn't mind sharing her beloved mountain.

"It'll be busy up here," Jesse said quietly.

"Of course," Lucy said. "It always is."

"So busy," Jesse said, "I reckon no one will even notice."

"Notice what?" Lucy asked impatiently.

"That I'm gone," Jesse replied.

15.

"Gone?" Lucy said softly. "What do you mean?"

Jesse looked out at the water. "I mean to leave here, Luce. I'm gonna run away that day. I can hide myself in one of them navy wagons, and by the time Pa realizes what I've done, it'll be too late. I'll be far off on a navy schooner."

Lucy sat down on the shore, thinking of all Jesse was saying—what it meant for Jesse, what it meant for her. Her head pounded.

"You're not saying much, Luce," Jesse said gently. He sat down next to her.

"I don't want you to go, Jess," she whispered, not trusting herself to say more. Just a short time ago she'd pictured him as a father, maybe as the father of her own children someday. Now she could only see him hidden away in one of the navy officer's wagons, buried in straw. She leaned her head against his shoulder, the idea of him gone too much to bear.

Jesse sighed. "I'll miss you, Lucy," he said. "And I'll miss Annie and Daniel and Polly and Grandpa and Ma and Joe and Sadie and Mary. But I gotta go, don't you see? I can't stay here, Luce. I'd curl up and die working the ironworks all my life."

Lucy said nothing She knew running away was what he thought he wanted. She knew he had this dream of the sea. She knew he would agonize over that dream every year when the navy returned, and most of the time in between. But she couldn't believe he wanted this more than anything else in life, more than the mountains, more than the idea of their lives staying the way they always had been, more than them being together forever.

"As for Samuel Lernley," Jesse said, "I promise you, Luce, I'll lose him for you before I leave. I got a few weeks to figure out a way to get rid of that guy, and I will."

But Lucy couldn't think of Samuel now. She could only think that she had just a few weeks left to be with Jesse. Maybe she should marry him, quickly before he left. Then he'd have to come back to her eventually. Would he do that? Would he want to? Would *she* want that—a life alone for years, childless but married to Jesse?

A plump, sweaty Daniel sat down in Lucy's lap. He looked up at her with sleepy eyes. "Hungry," Daniel said. "Daniel hungry."

Lucy hugged him to her, then she met Jesse's eyes and saw in them the sadness that was to come. She turned from Jesse and buried her face in Daniel's toddler body, letting his round little belly absorb her tears.

"Why are you crying, Lucy?" Annie's voice sounded behind Lucy, and Annie's arms wrapped around her neck.

"Jesse, why is Lucy crying?" Annie asked again.

Jesse didn't answer, and when Lucy looked up, his face was turned toward the water, away from Annie.

"What's wrong?" Annie asked.

"Nothing, nothing," Lucy said quickly, taking

Annie into her arms too. "Everything's all right, Annie. Everything's going to be all right."

They walked slowly back down the mountain to the village. At the road, Jesse stopped.

"We'll be heading on back, Lucy," Jesse said. "Ma said she can handle the young ones again and wants them to come home."

Lucy nodded. She would miss having Annie and Daniel and Polly at the house.

"Aw," Jesse groaned, kicking the road dust with his shoe. "I forgot I promised Ma I'd go check on Jenny Sims before I come home. Joseph's been asking for her, and Ma is fit to be tied that she hasn't come round after running out on them this morning."

"I'll go see Jenny for you," Lucy said quickly. "There's no need for you to have to drag the little ones up there."

"You sure, Luce?" Jesse asked.

Lucy nodded. There was no way that she wanted Jesse to go see about Jenny and discover the truth that she was ending her relationship with Joseph.

"All right. Thanks, Lucy," Jesse shouted back over

his shoulder as he and his siblings headed down the hill toward their house.

Slowly, Lucy climbed the hill toward her own home. She had supper to fix for her father. But her mind was awhirl now with what she was going to do about Jenny Sims.

She thought about it as she put some potatoes on to boil and tried to bake a pie, which didn't turn out right. She thought about it all through the quiet supper with her father. But no answer would come. And yet she knew she had to do something soon or Mrs. Rosseter would send Jesse back up to Jenny's. The Rosseters may not look for Jenny during supper, but they would expect her to come see Joseph sometime this evening.

As she was finishing up rinsing and drying the supper dishes, there was a soft knock on their front door.

"I'll see to it," Lucy's father called from the parlor.

There was the murmur of voices and the opening and closing of the screen door. Then her father was in the kitchen.

"Mr. Lernley would like to know if you would care to go for a stroll, Lucy," Lucy's father asked.

His eyes were twinkling with delight, and there was a part of her that wanted to say no, she wouldn't go. It annoyed her that her father had brought Samuel up on this subterfuge and thought she could not see through his plan. And yet the idea of staying at home, faced with her thoughts about Jenny and Jesse, seemed more than she could bear. An evening's walk in the summer air, even if it was with Samuel Lernley, seemed preferable to staying inside.

"All right," Lucy said, "I'll go."

Her father grinned, and Lucy scowled.

"This does not mean I like him, Father," she said sternly.

"Did I say that?" her father asked, widening his eyes in innocence.

"You didn't have to," Lucy said, throwing her dish-rag onto the washboard to dry. She untied her apron and went over to the looking glass. She smoothed back her hair and put on her cap, tucking a few loose strands back into place.

"You look very nice, Luce," her father said approvingly.

"I didn't ask you," Lucy said.

"That's all right," her father said. "I'm telling you just the same."

Giving him an annoyed glance, Lucy went out of the kitchen to the front door. Samuel was waiting on the porch, his hat in his hands, a lock of black hair falling onto his forehead. Lucy's stomach did an odd flip at the sight of him. She wondered if she wasn't getting herself into something that might be difficult to get out of.

"Glad you could join me, Miss Pettee," Samuel said.

Even with the noise of the blast furnace, it was a beautiful night. The sun was just beginning to set, its rays lighting the mountain around them in a pinkish glow.

"Shall we walk down toward the lake?" Samuel asked.

Lucy shook her head. "Let's not," she said. "It's too noisy there with the furnace and forges going. Let's walk back up the other side of the mountain and around to the upper lake. It'll be quieter there."

"The upper lake?" Samuel asked.

Lucy started, realizing that he didn't know about the two lakes and the way one fed into the other. He didn't know about the calmness and quietness of the upper lake, set as it was away from the ironworks. She knew that by taking him there she would be showing him a bit of her life, like opening a small crack in a door she had meant to keep shut. But somehow tonight that didn't matter.

"Come on," she said. "I'll show you."

They walked side by side, saying little. They climbed up the path to where a stream connected the upper and lower lakes, past the sawmill that lay quiet after a day's work.

When the path through the woods became too narrow, Samuel let Lucy lead the way. She moved ahead, conscious of him behind her, watching her. When she turned to hold out a branch that might have swung back and hit him, her eyes met his, and Lucy felt as if she had just immersed herself in cold water on a very hot day.

At one point, they were startled by a sound nearby, and stopped to watch two deer sniffing the air, their heads lifted.

"They sure are beautiful animals, Miss Pettee," Samuel whispered, standing close to her. "Don't see much of them in Boston."

The deer took flight at the sound of their voices.

"No, I guess you wouldn't," Lucy agreed, uncomfortably aware of the warmth of his body near hers.

Without much thought, Lucy led Samuel back to the Old Landing. Samuel whistled when he stood at the water's edge, looking out over the lake.

"Now, this is a place," Samuel said.

Lucy nodded. "It's Jess's and my spot," she said. "We used to sneak up here when we were trying to avoid our chores after school."

"Used to?" Samuel asked.

"Jesse works now," Lucy said, bending down to pick up a stone, and then sending it flying, "and we don't have much time for foolishness anymore."

Samuel smiled. "There should always be time for foolishness, Miss Pettee," he said. "At least *I* think so. I think there should be more foolishness the older you get. Without it, men and women turn mighty dull."

Lucy laughed, and Samuel laughed with her.

Then he looked back over the lake and sighed. "One could get used to a spot like this, Miss Pettee. Indeed one could have trouble leaving a place as beautiful as this."

Lucy nodded. "I would," she said.

"I can see that," Samuel said. "And I can see that I might have trouble leaving too, after a time."

Lucy looked in surprise at Samuel. "Are you finding our mountain to your liking, Mr. Lernley?" she asked.

"It's hard to get used to," he said slowly. "In Boston, there are so many people that you have more anonymity than here on the mountain."

Lucy laughed. "More?" she said. "Here you don't have *any*."

Samuel smiled. "That is true," he said. "And the noise is loud, but I like the beauty of it, the wildness of it. I like the people, too, and their different backgrounds and individuality. It's like a miniature world here."

Lucy hadn't thought of it like that, but in a way, he was right. There were proud Yankees and some wealthy gentry, Swiss and Lithuanians and Latvians and Swedes. They were a world unto themselves, as he'd said, and she liked this idea.

"Did you and Jesse bring the children here today?" Samuel asked, interrupting her thoughts. His voice had a funny edge to it.

Lucy nodded. "Yes," she said. "We swam here. Why?"

Samuel did not look at her for several moments. "I'm not sure how to ask this, Miss Pettee," he began, "so I guess I'll just go ahead and say it. Are you sweet on Jesse? I mean, is there more to you than friends?"

Samuel's face was red now as he waited for her answer.

"I don't know," Lucy said softly. "Jess is my best friend, Mr. Lernley. I've got no brothers or sisters, and he's like the brother I never had. Sometimes I think maybe there could be more, but how can you have something romantic with someone who is like your brother? It confuses me."

Lucy sighed. "I love Jesse. I always will. I don't

know if his plans for the future include me or not. Sometimes I hope they do."

Samuel blinked in surprise. "Th—Thank you for your honesty in this matter, Miss Pettee," he said, stammering. "If those are your feelings for him, then I guess there's not much else left to say but good evening."

He began to walk away, his chin up. Lucy watched him go, feeling bad that she had wounded his pride by telling him the truth. He marched determinedly up the path.

"Mr. Lernley," she finally called out.

Samuel continued on.

"Mr. Lernley," Lucy called again.

At this, Samuel turned toward her. Lucy smiled at him. "Mr. Lernley," she said, "I know you are determined to leave me behind, but you are on the wrong path. If you continue in that direction, you'll be headed for New York City."

Samuel grinned sheepishly, then he began to chuckle. Lucy giggled too. She liked that he could laugh at himself.

Samuel made his way back toward Lucy. "I guess I need your help to get back to Mrs. Brazee's."

Lucy nodded. She paused, looking at him thoughtfully, remembering his concern for her earlier. There was a side to Samuel Lernley that Lucy liked. He was responsible, a good man it seemed, one you might trust.

Lucy plunged ahead. "Actually, I could use your advice, if you're willing to listen."

"About what?" Samuel asked.

"Mrs. Rosseter was going to send Jesse to find Jenny Sims," Lucy said. "She's Joseph's fiancée, but I stopped Jess by saying I would go and see her. You see, Mr. Lernley, Jenny told me she's breaking it off with Joseph. And she asked me to tell Joseph for her. Now I have to go and explain why she hasn't come to see Joseph, but I don't know what to say."

Samuel grew grave. "Perhaps you should just try telling them the truth, Miss Pettee."

Lucy smiled slightly. "Like I did with you just now?"

Samuel grimaced. "Yes," he said. "Joseph may be stronger than you think. And lying has never solved anything for anyone."

"I have to do it tonight," she said softly.

Samuel put his hand on Lucy's arm. "Let's get it done, then, Miss Pettee," he said. "I always believe in meeting unpleasant things head-on and getting them over with."

Lucy nodded, yet she still felt a reluctance to go.

"I'll wait for you outside," Samuel said. "It might help to talk about it afterward, if you like."

"I would appreciate that," Lucy said, realizing she truly meant it. It would be good to have someone waiting for her when she had finished this unpleasant task.

"You know," Samuel said slowly, "your sharing this with me has changed my mind, Miss Pettee. I am not giving up on you, after all.

"Besides," he added, grinning, "I've always enjoyed a little competition."

Samuel took her arm, and Lucy felt herself grow warm. She was pleased somehow that she had not completely driven him away.

Still, she worried about what she had done. How could she overlook her growing feelings for Jesse? Was she being cruel in leading Samuel to believe there could be something between them? Had she started something now that she would have to end unhappily?

Once again, Lucy cursed herself for not thinking before she'd acted. She was in a pickle once more as a result. Samuel was walking beside her, confident now that she had confided in him. And yet they were headed to the Rosseters' and to Jesse, the boy who had her heart. What had she gotten herself into?

16.

"Lucy! Lucy's here!" Annie yelled from the front porch, where she sat in the growing darkness.

"Hello, Annie," Lucy said softly.

"And it's Samuel!" Annie shouted. "Samuel's here too!"

Annie flew from the porch and into Samuel's arms. He grunted in surprise at her swift flight but caught her and swung her up into the air. Annie shrieked with delight.

Jesse stepped out onto the porch. He eyed Samuel with suspicion.

"I need to talk to you and your Ma," Lucy said.

"Why?" Jesse asked. "What's wrong?"

"Go on, Miss Pettee," Samuel said. "I can take care of Annie, and you can send Daniel on out if he's still up."

Mrs. Rosseter came out onto the porch too. "He's asleep, thank the Lord," she said. "But I appreciate the offer just the same, Mr. Lernley. I've heard a great deal about you the past few hours. Annie talks of little else."

"Children are easily impressed," Samuel said, laughing.

"Not Annie," Mrs. Rosseter said.

"Can we talk, Mrs. Rosseter?" Lucy asked, wanting this to be over.

"All right, Lucy," Mrs. Rosseter said, her smile fading quickly when she saw how serious Lucy was. "Come on in."

"You needn't wait," Jesse said to Samuel. "I can take Lucy home."

"Now, Jess," Mrs. Rosseter said, "Mr. Lernley has offered to watch over Annie so we can talk. Don't be acting so uppish." She turned to Samuel. "We'll be in the kitchen should you need us."

"Happy to help, ma'am," Samuel said, tipping his hat and then taking it off completely to set it on Annie's head. Annie crowed and began strutting around the front yard.

Lucy followed Mrs. Rosseter and Jesse inside. Grandpa was sitting at the kitchen table. Would she have to shout the news out so that Grandpa could hear?

But Mrs. Rosseter seemed to know that this was to be a private conversation. "Come, Pa," she said loudly. "Let me take you into the front room by the fire. A new book arrived yesterday at Lucy's father's store, and I picked it up for you. It's called *Frankenstein,* and I hear the author, Mary Shelley, is wonderful."

"Never heard of her," Grandpa yelled out.

"I know," Mrs. Rosseter yelled back as she helped Grandpa from his chair. "She's new, Pa."

"I like the classics," Grandpa yelled.

"Well," Mrs. Rosseter yelled back, "you might want to try this one just for something different, Pa."

Jesse and Lucy were alone in the kitchen.

"I thought you didn't like that guy," Jesse grumbled, "but every time I turn around you're with him."

Lucy didn't say anything. Did she like him? Didn't she like him? She was so confused. And what about Jesse? Why didn't he tell her what was in *his* heart?

Mrs. Rosseter came back into the kitchen. "Sit down, Lucy," she said. "You obviously have bad news, and I don't want to make you stand while you deliver it."

Lucy took a chair, and Jesse sat next to her.

Lucy cleared her throat. "You remember this morning when Jenny Sims came here?" she asked.

"Yes," Mrs. Rosseter said.

Lucy sighed. "After she ran out, I followed her, Mrs. Rosseter. She . . ."

From the other room, Joseph moaned. Mrs. Rosseter got up and softly closed the door to the kitchen.

"Go on, Lucy," Mrs. Rosseter said.

"Oh, Mrs. Rosseter," Lucy finally blurted out, "Jenny Sims is breaking off her engagement to Joe. She couldn't face Joseph's injuries."

"And she couldn't come tell us that herself?" Mrs. Rosseter said, her mouth puckering in disapproval.

Lucy shook her head.

"Glory be," Jesse said. "How could that ninny do that to our Joe? I knew she was stupid, but I didn't reckon she was heartless."

Mrs. Rosseter's voice was tight. "Maybe she weren't so insensitive, Jesse. Maybe breaking it off with our Joe was the only thing she could do. Maybe if she'd stayed with Joseph, she would have been less than useless, and that's not what Joseph needs."

"But Ma—," Jesse started.

"I know," Mrs. Rosseter interrupted. "This is gonna hurt your brother a great deal." She looked down at the floor.

"I'll tell him for you if you want, Mrs. Rosseter," Lucy said. "Jenny did ask me to."

Mrs. Rosseter raised her head. "No, Lucy," she said. "I must tell him. It's been hard enough on you, I imagine, being left with having to tell me."

Just then, Mr. Rosseter walked into the kitchen. He looked at them all questioningly.

"Wonder if he'll still think Joe should have been at that furnace *now*," Jesse muttered.

"Enough, Jesse," Mrs. Rosseter said.

She walked over to her husband. "Jenny Sims won't be coming to see Joe."

"Is she coming tomorrow?" her husband said.

"No, she ain't coming at all," Mrs. Rosseter said.

"She's left him?" he asked, his eyes widening in surprise.

Mrs. Rosseter nodded.

"Dear Lord," Mr. Rosseter said in a strangled voice.

"I'm going in now to tell Joseph," Mrs. Rosseter said. She walked from her husband and put a hand on Lucy's shoulder.

"That was hard, I know," she said, "but I do thank you for coming to give us her message, Lucy. Your delivering it made it easier."

Then Mr. Rosseter was beside his wife. "You'll not do this alone," he said firmly. "It's best if we go together. I'll tell him. You hold him."

Mrs. Rosseter smiled sadly at her husband, and they left the room.

"Poor Joe. Nice of the old man to give him the news, though," Jesse said bitterly.

Lucy scooted her chair close to Jesse and wrapped her arms around him.

"Oh, Jess," she whispered, "please, please, think about it a minute. Joe wanted to work the furnace. He always has. If you really intend to leave soon, or even if you plan to stay, make peace with your pa. Please."

Jesse looked at her, surprised.

"I know," Lucy said. "I've always understood how you didn't get along, but lately, Jesse . . . I don't know. Everything seems so upside down. Believe me, Jess, your pa is broken up about this. And you don't want to continue on with bad feelings between you, do you?"

"Luce," Jesse said, his voice gruff, "you're going soft on me."

"Maybe I am. But will you think on it?"

Jesse nodded. "I will, but only if you'll think on what the heck it is you're after with Samuel Lernley. Deal?" He spit on his hand and held it up. "After all, I don't want to spend my last few weeks making plans on how to get rid of the chap if you're just gonna bring him back after I leave. And I do mean to get rid of him. He ain't the one for you, Lucy."

Lucy spit on her palm and rubbed it with Jesse's, but she was angry for a minute as they made their pact. If Samuel wasn't the one for her, who did Jesse think was? If he thought she should wait for *him*, why didn't he speak up and tell her so?

Jesse saw her to the door and out into the evening's darkness.

"You know you shouldn't be going home in the dark without a chaperone," he said. "There'll be talk if you're caught."

"I've been out plenty of times with you and no one else," Lucy said tartly, still feeling confused and a bit angry.

"I ain't Samuel Lernley," he whispered in her ear as they approached Samuel and Annie.

Lucy wished he was. It would make everything so much simpler.

Samuel smiled when he saw Lucy, and lowered Annie back to the ground from where he had been holding her high.

"Does he gotta leave?" Annie asked, turning to Lucy.

"I'm afraid I do," Samuel said. "I promised Miss Pettee I'd see her home."

"Jess can do that," Annie said, "and you can stay and play."

"Another time, Annie," Jesse said, scooping up his sister. "It's time for bed for you, anyway."

"I hate you," Annie said.

"How come you say you hate me when I tell you it's time for bed, but you say you love me when I take you swimming?" Jesse asked.

"'Cause *then* I love you," Annie said. She buried her face in her brother's shoulder. "Actually, I always love you, Jess," she said.

"I always love you, too, Annie," he said, his voice cracking. "Remember that."

Jesse's eyes met Lucy's. Her throat felt like a hand was pressing on it.

"Night, Samuel," Jesse said stiffly.

"Good night, Jesse," Samuel replied.

Samuel held out his arm, and Lucy took it. Together they walked away.

When they were out of earshot, Samuel bent his head toward Lucy's.

"Are you all right?" he asked.

"As all right as I can be," Lucy responded, her voice thick with emotion. "Mr. and Mrs. Rosseter are in telling Joseph now."

"Then you didn't have to do it yourself?" Samuel asked.

Lucy shook her head.

"I'm glad," Samuel said.

As they passed Grandma Brazee's house, Lucy heard the creak of her rocker and felt like groaning.

"Lucy Pettee," she shouted out. "Who's that you've got with you? That don't sound like Jesse Rosseter to me."

"It's Samuel Lernley, Grandma," Lucy said.

"It's mighty dark to be out alone with Mr. Lernley, Lucy," Grandma Brazee warned. "Ain't your father taught you nothing?"

"We're on our way home, Grandma," Lucy said. "We stopped at the Rosseters' first."

"What for?" Grandma's voice was sharp. "You seeing two lads now?"

Lucy was glad that the night was dark. She knew her face was hot with embarrassment.

"No, Grandma," she said. "We have to hurry. My father's expecting us."

"Well now, Mr. Lernley," Grandma called out. "You go and get that girl on home, but hurry back here. I want to hear how they're doing down at the Rosseters' house, and there's a bat in my kitchen I'd like you to take a broom to."

"Yes, ma'am," Samuel called back.

"Gossipy old bag," Lucy whispered to Samuel.

"Try living with her," Samuel said.

Lucy laughed. "No, thank you."

When they got to Lucy's porch, they stood outside for a minute. Samuel reached down and took Lucy's hands.

"Thank you, Miss Pettee, for taking me to the upper lake," he said. "It was a beautiful spot, and in spite of some things said, I enjoyed it."

Lucy nodded. "Thank you for waiting for me at the Rosseters'."

Samuel nodded.

"Good night, then," Lucy said.

"Miss Pettee?"

Lucy turned.

"I was wondering if you might consider accompanying me to the ball at the Proving Ceremony?" Samuel asked, hope in his voice. "If you haven't been asked already?"

Lucy hesitated. She couldn't say no after what she had said to him tonight and how good he had been to her. Besides, Jesse would have too many things on his mind in the coming weeks to ask her.

"Yes, Mr. Lernley," she said. "I would be happy to go with you."

But as she said it, she wondered if "happy" was the right word. How could she be happy, knowing what was to happen that night at the ceremony?

17.

The day of the Proving Ceremony dawned clear, bright, and colder than usual for an October day. Lucy leaned out her bedroom window, drinking in the sunshine and listening to the last sounds of the furnace, which would shut down that night with the dance. She could smell the first hint of winter fast approaching and felt a shiver from the cool breeze of the morning. While she had once welcomed the end of the iron season and the quiet that would come when it was over, she could now only think about what this winter would be like without Jesse by her side. She imagined the lonely days in school and the long, dark evenings alone with only her father for company. She thought of the evening visits, the quilting sessions, the banjo playing and fiddling and dancing without Jesse. How was she to bear it?

She hadn't seen much of Jesse these past weeks. He was working at the furnace constantly. But she had helped gather things for his escape: a knit hat, warm wool socks, a few coins. Each of these things she had hidden near the Old Landing in a spot they had chosen together. Every time she laid another item down in the hole they had dug, she saw that the pile was growing and that Jesse's leaving time was nearer.

Once when she had hurried to the upper lake with some canned fish, she felt a touch on her back as she was kneeling down to bury it. Jesse was standing there, some clothes slung over his shoulder.

He had not said a word but had put his arms around her when she'd stood. She had buried her face in his chest, wanting him to say something. But when she had finally pulled away and looked at him, he'd turned his face from her.

"Are you crying, Jesse Rosseter?" she had asked.

"No," he responded huffily. "That perfume you've taken to wearing makes me gag."

Lucy laughed.

Then Jesse had put some shirts down in the hiding

spot. When he stood, he faced her. "I liked you best when you smelled of woods and smoke and natural things. Who told you that perfume smells good?"

Lucy didn't answer.

"Samuel!" Jesse accused her. "Samuel Lernley likes you in perfume."

"He'd like me without perfume too," Lucy responded hotly.

Jesse let out an angry snort. "I reckon he would! But now the question is, do you like Samuel with or without perfume?"

"What a stupid question, Jesse Rosseter," Lucy said just as angrily. "Without, of course."

She stomped her foot when she realized what she'd just said. "Oh, I hate you, I really do. I'm glad you're going. You're a nuisance, anyway."

Jesse grabbed her shoulders. "I am going. But I ain't about to leave with you making some big mistake."

"What choice do I have?" Lucy argued.

"Any choice you want," Jesse said.

Lucy looked down at the ground then. "I choose for you to stay," she said softly.

Jesse hugged her to him again. "I wish I could Luce," he whispered. "Please say you understand. I couldn't bear it if you . . ."

"If I what?" she asked. Say *something,* she willed him.

"I just gotta go," Jesse said. "You see that, don't you?"

Lucy cried. *No,* she thought, *I don't see it. Why do you have to go?*

The memory of that afternoon had haunted her for days.

Now, looking out the window, Lucy's thoughts turned to Samuel. She had seen him often lately, mainly with her father, and what she had seen she had liked. He wasn't Jesse. It wasn't always comfortable with him. He wasn't like an old shoe, worn and familiar, but he made her feel something different. The feeling was a strange one, kind of wild and scary, the same way she had felt on the day she'd jumped into the lake from the cliff with Jesse—frightened but exhilarated.

She turned from the window and looked at the dress her father had given her for the Proving

Ceremony. Its brown taffeta and white lace collar and cuffs shone new and crisp on her quilt. It was a beautiful dress, the prettiest she had ever owned. She knew Samuel would be taken with her in it, and that pleased her. But still, it was a bittersweet pleasure knowing that her night out with Samuel would be mingled with Jesse's leaving her behind.

"Lucy," her father called from downstairs, "there are chores to be done today!"

"Coming, Father," Lucy called back. She was about to go, when she caught sight of Jesse at the edge of the forest. He was standing stock still, gazing at her house.

Lucy lifted a hand and waved, but he didn't see her. Instead he turned and walked slowly away. Lucy watched him go and wondered at Jesse's manner. Could it be possible he was changing his mind, now that the time to leave had really come? Or was his desire to go to sea so great it could overcome his love of this mountain? And of her? Lucy wanted to chase after him and see if perhaps he was wavering in his decision.

"Lucy!" her father called sharply.

She sighed. The question would have to wait until tonight. She closed her shutters against the cold and went to do her chores.

That evening Lucy drank in the beauty of the torch-lit village green, the lower lake gleaming in the moonlight, the soft sweet sound of fiddles being played. Before her was a large crowd of people dressed in their best for the evening. Lucy leaned into Samuel's arm, and he smiled down at her.

"Have I told you how breathtaking you look tonight?" he asked.

"About a hundred times," she teased him.

"A hundred and one now," he said. He squeezed her arm, and Lucy felt the heat from his hand.

She moved with him toward the crowd. There were many people there from down off the mountain whom Lucy didn't know, everyone waiting for the men from the navy to arrive. Lucy realized that this was what it would be like to live in Boston, surrounded by unfamiliar people. She felt a brief moment of panic, and wondered if she should be with Samuel at all. What was she encouraging?

Did she want this? Then a familiar voice sounded behind her.

"Done your choosing, then, missy?"

Grandma Brazee sat in a rocker. Someone must have brought it for her from her house to the green. She was dressed in finery like everyone else there, but had managed to maintain her mountain demeanor with a chicken's feather stuck in her hair. Next to her sat Grandpa Rosseter.

"Good evening, Grandma Brazee," Lucy said politely, ignoring Grandma's comment. "Hello, Grandpa," she yelled.

"Well, you got a good one there, missy," Grandma said, winking at Samuel, "even if he takes a bit long when bathing in the tub in my kitchen. Almost didn't have time to bake the pies I bring every year to the ceremony, he was so long about it."

Lucy swallowed her laugh, seeing Samuel trying desperately to ignore Grandma by seeming interested in something far away.

"I've always liked clean men, Grandma," Lucy said. "My father takes a long bath himself."

"Don't remember you minding too much when

Jesse was at his dirtiest, missy," Grandma said tartly.

"What's this about baths?" Grandpa yelled, cupping his ear.

Several people turned to look at them.

Now it was Lucy's turn to be embarrassed. She was about to respond, when there was a loud cheer from just beyond the green. The wagons were arriving with at least twenty naval officers in each one, their coats pressed and buttons gleaming.

The wagons circled the green, and then stopped for a moment while the officers jumped from the wagons to the ground, eyeing the young girls, who eyed them back. The Proving Ceremony always brought about at least one wedding and more than a handful of drunken brawls.

Lucy watched the wagons pull off to a spot where darkness would provide enough cover for Jesse to sneak into one. *Which one would he ride away in?* she wondered. *In which wagon would he leave her?*

Then she spied Sadie in among the crowd that surrounded the officers, talking to one of them, sashaying back and forth. Lucy looked around but didn't see Jesse or Mr. and Mrs. Rosseter near Sadie.

"Samuel," Lucy said, "come with me. I think we'd better do some chaperoning."

"*We* have to chaperone?" Samuel asked, raising his eyebrows. "Do you consider me as safe as all that?"

Lucy laughed. "No," she said, "but I think Sadie Rosseter by herself with a naval officer is just a bit more dangerous!"

They walked over to Sadie, who, on noticing them, stepped away from the navy man. "Hey, Lucy," she said. "Mr. Lernley."

"Where are your folks, Sadie?" Lucy asked.

"They're coming shortly," she said. "They're helping Joseph over to the ladder of the tripod. He's to help drop the anchors."

"Ah," Lucy said, happy to know that Joseph was up and about. Though he was stronger these past few weeks, Joseph had not ventured out of the Rosseter house much. Lucy was glad Joseph was going to join the party tonight, and glad that Jenny was nowhere around. Her parents had sent her to visit a distant cousin for a while, hoping the mountain folks' criticism of her behavior would lessen with her absence.

"Hello," said the naval officer who had been talking to Sadie. He stuck his hand out to Samuel and introduced himself.

Samuel shook the officer's hand.

The officer smiled at them all. "Sure is a long way up this mountain," he said. "Don't you ever get lonely way up here?"

"Oh, yes," Sadie said. "It can get very lonesome, especially in the winter."

"But there isn't a lovelier spot on Earth than this mountain when it snows," Lucy protested.

"Lucy's a little mad," Sadie said, grinning. "She likes it when we are all shut in up here."

"I don't think she's crazy," Samuel said quietly. "I've only been here two months, but I can see the hold a place like this might have on a person, even with the snow."

"Yes," the naval officer said, looking around at the green and the lake. "I think I agree with you, sir. Even though it is mighty remote, this mountain has some charm."

He glanced at Sadie. "Especially if the company

of ladies such as these were possible through that long winter."

Sadie giggled, and Lucy cleared her throat.

The officer grinned and bowed. "No offense meant, miss."

Lucy smiled at him. It was hard for her to act so prim and proper, and yet she had to be sure Sadie didn't get in any trouble tonight, or go running off with this officer. The Rosseters would hardly need that added worry.

"They're raising the first one! They're raising it!" Shouts came from across the green.

"An anchor's going up," Lucy said. "Shall we go join the rest of the crowd and see how it does in the dropping?"

Samuel nodded and took Lucy's arm. The naval officer held out his arm for Sadie, who took it, smiling widely.

"Don't worry," Samuel assured Lucy. "I won't let them out of our sights."

They followed the rest of the crowd to the bottom of a large iron tripod that had been erected near the lake just for this occasion. In the light from the torches, Lucy could see that the first anchor had been raised to the top and fastened with ropes. A few cuts would slice the ropes, and the anchor would fall to the ground.

After months of work at the furnace, this was a big night for all the ironworkers. If the anchors held and proved themselves, the furnace and forges would still be in business next year. If more than one or two of the anchors didn't do well, the reputation of the ironworkers would be tarnished. Every year the community held its breath, hoping all of the anchors would prove sound. Never had more than one or two of them broken, although the mountain folk had heard horror stories of other iron-forging communities that had not been so lucky.

Lucy watched as Joseph climbed the ladder of the tripod. He climbed slowly and stiffly and did not smile. She wished with all her might that these anchors might prove the strongest ever made on the mountain—if for no other reason than for Joe.

Joseph raised his knife to cut the ropes holding the first anchor in place. Everyone began to cheer. Samuel smiled at Lucy.

Men from the mountain pushed the crowd back to prevent anyone from getting hurt. Joseph bent over, and someone else held the ropes steady while he began to cut. His good arm moved steadily back and forth.

Just then Lucy felt a warm hand slip into hers. Jesse was by her side. He was here!

There was a loud snap as, at last, the ropes gave way. And with a swift rush of wind and a cry from those below, the anchor fell to the ground.

18.

The anchor landed with a crash. It turned and fell heavily on its side, but it held.

A cheer rose from the crowd. Several naval officers grabbed women near them and swung them high. The women shrieked with laughter. One by one the anchors were dropped, each one of them holding steady. The Proving Ceremony was a success.

When the last anchor had been dropped and the inspecting admiral had punch-stamped each one, proclaiming the anchors fit, the festivities began. The fiddlers put their fiddles to their chins and burst out with a merry tune.

From the tripod high above them, Joseph began his stiff climb back down the ladder. He reached the bottom and slowly walked away from the crowd, toward home. Mrs. Rosseter hurried after him and tried to urge him back to the festivities, but he shook his head and went on walking alone into the dark, away from the light and noise.

"He'll never be the same," Jesse said softly, his voice bitter.

Lucy was afraid Jesse might be right, but she didn't want to think about it. "Give him some time, Jess," she said. "He'll heal."

Jesse shook his head. "Maybe," he said. "Maybe not. I won't be here to see."

Lucy squeezed Jesse's hand tightly. "Are you sure?" she whispered. *Change your mind,* she thought, *change your mind.*

But Jesse nodded.

"Well," Samuel said, smiling at them both, unaware of what was being said between them, "it looks as if the mountain will be in business for the next year. Shall we celebrate with the others and dance, Miss Pettee?"

How could she celebrate when Jesse was leaving? "Actually, Luce promised me the first dance, didn't you, Lucy?" Jesse said.

Lucy's breath caught at Jesse's words. The night

was to be Samuel's with her, but she couldn't say no to Jesse when he was leaving.

If only she could tell Samuel and justify her actions. Lucy swallowed hard. She knew it was wrong to leave Samuel, but still, she put out her hand for Jesse. She didn't look back. She couldn't bear to see how Samuel was taking her betrayal.

Jesse led her to the center of the green, in among the other dancers. The band was playing a waltz, and Jesse took her in his arms and swung her around on the grass.

"You look mighty good tonight," he said mockingly. "*Samuel* must be pleased."

"Oh, I don't think he's too pleased at all right now," Lucy said. "I am dancing with *you,* remember?"

Jesse frowned. "He'll get over it."

"But will I?" Lucy said. "Oh, Jess," she sighed, putting her head on his shoulder. "Are you sure about this? Really sure?"

"Yes, Lucy," Jesse said. "I'm sure."

"Don't you care about me, Jess?" Lucy asked.

"Of course I do," he said lightly.

"Then stay," Lucy begged.

"Maybe . . . ," Jesse began, and he paused.

Maybe? Maybe what?

"I can't." Jesse shook his head.

"Can't what?" Lucy demanded.

Jesse pulled her so close, she almost couldn't breathe.

"I'll come back, Luce," Jesse said, his voice cracking. "Will you . . ."

"Will I what, Jess?" Lucy asked impatiently, daring him to say it. "What?"

With a sudden spurt of energy, Jesse wheeled her around the green and into the shadows by the woods. Before Lucy could say a word, he had taken her face in his hands and put his lips on hers. The unfamiliar feeling made Lucy's knees go weak, made her breath short, and gave her a rush she had never felt before. She willed him to go on kissing her forever until she molded completely with him. But he pulled away, leaving her gasping for breath.

"Will you be here if I come back?" Jesse asked abruptly. "Or will Samuel take you away?"

"Oh, Jess," Lucy pleaded, swaying unsteadily, "just stay here with me."

Jesse looked away, but not before Lucy saw the indecision there.

She had her answer. He had kissed her, and he was still unsure about staying. Well, then, she would make the leaving easy for him.

"You'd best write me, then, when you're good and gone," she said angrily. "And if I hear you've turned buccaneer, I'll search you out on the high seas myself."

Jesse said nothing, but she saw his body stiffen. Abruptly, he pulled her to him again and danced her back into the light.

Lucy glanced over at Samuel, who looked in astonishment at her coming out of the woods with Jesse. He turned and strode away from the crowd.

"But perhaps," she whispered to herself, "I just *might* be here when you return years from now, after all."

And for once, the thought of her life on hold, waiting for Jesse, wasn't as pleasant as it had been in the past.

Lucy finished one more dance with Jesse. When it was over, his fingers brushed her cheek, but he did not kiss her again. Lucy was glad. She didn't think she could bear it.

"Gotta go grab a last dance with Ma," he said softly. "Then I'll be hiding myself in one of them wagons to go."

He dropped his arm from Lucy's waist, and she reluctantly backed away.

"I'll think of you every day, Luce," he whispered to her.

Lucy watched him wander through the crowds. He found his mother and asked her to dance, and Lucy saw the pleasure on his mother's face. The two of them swung around the green until the dance was finished.

Jesse hugged his mother and kissed her on the cheek. He caught Lucy's eye, spit on his hand, and raised his palm to her. She lifted hers to match his. And then Jesse disappeared into the darkness of the woods where the navy wagons were waiting.

Lucy wanted to go home now that Jesse had left. She wanted to go upstairs, take her dress off, fall into bed, and wrap herself up in a quilt where she could cry for as long as she wanted. But there was Samuel to think about. He had been so anxious for this night, and she had let him down by dancing with Jesse.

By tomorrow Samuel would know why she had taken that dance, but for now, Lucy wanted to try to make the rest of the evening right for him.

"Lucy!" her father called.

Lucy went over to where her father stood with some other men, drinking beer out of barrels.

"Haven't seen much of you, honey," her father said. "Where's Samuel got off to?"

"I'm not sure," Lucy said.

Abram Ostrander spoke up. "You looking for Samuel Lernley?" he asked.

"Yes," Lucy said.

"Saw him going off toward the lake," Mr. Ostrander said. "Seemed like he was pretty angry, Luce. You give him all those dark thoughts, young lady?" Mr. Ostrander winked at her.

Her father regarded her closely. "Everything all right, Luce?" he asked quietly.

Lucy shrugged. "I'm not sure, Father," she said. "It may be that Mr. Lernley is a little bit upset with me."

"Why would that be?" her father asked. "You haven't done anything unseemly, have you?"

"Just been dancing with Jesse," Nathaniel Sherwood said. "Guess it would upset any man who'd brung a girl to a dance to see her dancing with someone else."

Her father looked at her severely.

"I'll—I'll go and try to find Samuel," was all that Lucy managed to stammer out.

Lucy wandered all around the green, in and out among the crowd, but Samuel was nowhere to be found. She walked to the edge of the lower lake, hoping he'd be there, but he wasn't. When she got back to where her father was still standing, he put his arm around her shoulder and moved her away from the other men.

"If you've been trifling with Samuel," her father said softly, "then it'd be better if you left him alone right now."

Lucy felt hot tears coming to her eyes. Jesse was leaving, Samuel was upset, and her father was angry too. At the moment, Lucy had no way to make any of it right.

Suddenly there was screaming and yelling behind the dancers. The crowd parted, and Mr. Rosseter came out from the woods, dragging Jesse by the collar.

"I'll tan your hide when we get home!" Mr. Rosseter was yelling.

The music stopped. Everyone was staring.

"Reckon you'll run away on me, do you?" Mr. Rosseter shouted. "I'll teach you better. You're my son, and my son ain't running away to no navy!"

Mr. Rosseter dragged Jesse across the green, Jesse fighting him tooth and nail.

Understanding dawned in Lucy's father's eyes.

"Problem, Edward?" Eric Moseman had gone to confront Mr. Rosseter.

"Found him trying to hide in one of them wagons," Mr. Rosseter said, gritting his teeth. "Trying to run away to that navy he says he wants to join so badly."

"So why not let him go, then, Edward?" Mr. Moseman said reasonably.

Jesse stopped fighting. He looked hopefully at his father.

"Ain't your business, Eric," Mr. Rosseter said. "I

make the decisions in my own family, and I won't brook no interference. You ain't got no children, so you wouldn't understand."

At this, Jesse wrenched himself around and broke free. He pushed through the crowd, moving fast. Without even a backward glance, he ran.

"Now see what you done?" Mr. Rosseter yelled at Mr. Moseman. "He's free again, and I gotta go chasing after him."

He turned to the crowd. "Hey," he said, "will some of you men come help me get him?"

Mrs. Rosseter was beside him now. "Edward," she said softly, "let him go. He don't want to stay here, can't you see that?"

"It's not about what he wants," Mr. Rosseter said to her. "It's about a family remaining together as they should. Jesse'll stay on this mountain and work the furnace like we all do up here. I ain't listening to anything more about it."

He turned toward the crowd. "Now, who here's gonna help me search?"

Several men stepped forward to volunteer, but others looked away. Lucy was not surprised by those who volunteered. They were men who ran strict households in which they ruled, like Mr. Rosseter.

"Come on, then," Mr. Rosseter said, motioning to the men who had stepped forward to help. "We'll divide up for the search."

The men split up and left, while the rest of the crowd milled around. The celebration seemed to have died off.

"Let's go home, Luce," her father said softly beside her.

Lucy followed her father. She walked with him up the front porch steps and into the hallway. There in the darkness, her father paused.

"I'm sorry about Jesse, Lucy," he said.

"Me too," Lucy said softly. "I didn't mean to hurt Samuel's feelings."

Her father nodded. "I can see that now."

"I'll find him tomorrow and explain," Lucy said.

"Somehow I think he'll understand," her father said.

He lit a candle, and together they climbed the stairs. At the top, her father kissed her on the forehead.

"Good night, Lucy," he said.

"Good night, Father," she replied.

Her father entered his room and shut the door, taking the candle with him. Lucy was left in the darkness, listening to the silence of the mountain, so strange after months of the furnace running strong.

Oh, Jess, she thought, *if only I could help you now.*

19.

Two hours later, bells began to ring wildly on the green. Doors could be heard slamming madly, and horse hooves pounded on the dirt road outside Lucy's house.

Lucy threw a wrapper around her nightgown and tried to still her rapid breathing before throwing the door open to the hallway. Her father came out, his hair disheveled, stumbling a bit after being pulled from sleep.

"Lucy? What's happening?" he asked.

"It sounds as if the town is going crazy," Lucy said.

She followed her father down the front porch steps and out into the night.

Men and women were hurrying past them, buckets in their hands.

"Nate," Lucy's father called out to Betsy Sherwood's father. "What is it? What's happened?"

"Fire!" Mr. Sherwood yelled back. "Fire in the meadow. The woods are mighty dry, Jonathan. Could be bad."

"Lucy, grab those buckets by the back porch steps," her father said. "You'll have to head to the lake with the women and children."

Lucy hurried to the back porch, the blood pounding in her ears. Dry, Mr. Sherwood had said. She hadn't thought about it, but the woods *were* awfully dry. It had hardly rained at all this summer. What if the fire in the meadow got out of control? What if it worked its way toward the mountain and the furnace? The entire livelihood of the mountain could be lost in one horrific blaze.

The idea was too terrible to consider. Lucy grabbed the buckets. She'd go and help as soon as she put something decent on and made one quick stop—one stop to be sure.

"Here, Lucy," her father said, holding out his hand and taking his bucket. "Go help out at the lake, and stay away from the fire."

"Yes, Father," Lucy said. "Don't worry about me. I'll be all right."

"If that fire gets out of control, Lucy, get into the lake," her father said. "You hear me?"

Lucy had a sudden picture of flames engulfing the mountain, destroying everything in its path.

"Go, Father," Lucy said. "Hurry."

Lucy flew up the stairs to her room. She threw on a faded gown and cap. She buttoned up her oldest boots and ran outside into the night to help.

Black smoke filled the air. The smell of it hung heavy in the night.

Lucy raced past Grandma Brazee's, which was deserted. Already the old woman and Samuel must be somewhere helping with the efforts to put out the fire.

Now, in the collier meadow, she could make out flames leaping into the air. She needed to hurry and help the others. Just one stop first.

She entered the Rosseter house without knocking. Jesse's family would not be there. They, too, would be helping, one way or another. *But,* she thought, *maybe Jesse'll have come back.*

In the quiet of the house, she heard a small sound. She walked toward the bedrooms, and there Jesse stood, a bundle on the bed next to him.

He looked up quickly, with guilt. His eyes softened when he saw her.

"You'd better hurry," Lucy said. "They'll be urging the naval officers to move the wagons on down the mountain."

There was suddenly uncertainty in his eyes. "But the fire—"

"Go, Jess," she said. "Don't let this happen in vain. Use the fire to finally go."

"But I can't leave . . . if the fire . . ." He paused. "What if someone gets hurt?"

"Someone?" Lucy asked in exasperation. "*Who*, Jesse? *Who* are you worried about?"

He stared at her. "You," he finally whispered.

She went toward him then, threw her arms around his neck, and pressed herself strongly up against him. "Then stay," she said. "Stay and keep me safe, forever."

He gave an uneasy laugh. "Me keep *you* safe, Lucy?" he joked. "You're the one girl I know that could arm wrestle a bear if she wanted."

Lucy let her arms drop. He had kissed her at the dance tonight. There was no denying that. They could not go back to that old jocular relationship. He could leave, or he could stay, but she would know how he felt—tonight!

"Enough, Jess," she said. "No more. Stay and marry me, or go quickly. There is no more time to waiver. You have to choose."

"But . . ." He paused.

"Choose," she shouted at him.

He looked at her for a moment, then his glance slid away to the window. "I gotta . . . I can't . . ." He couldn't finish.

Lucy saw the situation clearly in that moment. How was Jesse supposed to choose? Could he really decide between the girl he loved and the life he wanted? Could she truly stand there, loving him, and force him to make that choice? *Sometimes,* Lucy realized, *love isn't about what is right for you.*

"Go," she said softly.

Jesse picked up his bundle. He hesitated.

Lucy stood still as stone. "I said go, Jesse," she said fiercely.

In one quick step, he was beside her and had gathered her to him.

"I'll come back," he whispered.

Lucy shook her head. "We've always had honesty between us," she said, the tears already starting to come. "Let's keep it that way, Jess."

"I do love you, Luce," he choked out.

"I know."

He pulled her tighter against him and bent to kiss her again. But Lucy put her fingers on his lips, stopping him. "No, Jess," she said. "Let's not end it like that."

He stared at her. Lucy looked away.

She had made the right choice. He had said he loved her, but even that love couldn't keep him here. She knew that if he stayed, he would eventually hate her for it.

Lucy leaned her head against Jesse's shoulder, and smelled his woody smell for the very last time. She ran her fingers over his face as if that would help her to remember. A tear ran down Jesse's cheek, and she wiped it away and smiled at him. He turned then and left the room. She listened as he walked down the hall and out of the house, shutting the door softly behind him. He was gone.

Lucy sat down on his bed. Her hands began to shake, and then her body shook too, and the tears came hard. They wracked her body. Her shoulders trembled with the force of her loss.

She cried and cried until she was too weak to cry anymore.

Then, at last, she stood. She took a deep breath and squared her shoulders. He was gone. It was over. Now it was time to go help put out the fire.

As Lucy approached the lower lake, she could see that the flames in the meadow near the collier's charcoal pits were moving quickly. She was shocked at how large the fire had become just since she had gone to the Rosseters', and how it seemed to be growing faster than anyone could get water to it. She hurried to help the others, her heart pounding. The older ones and the children stood knee-deep in the lake, making escape easier for them should it be necessary.

There were two lines, one line filling bucket after bucket from the lake and then passing it hand to hand on down the line toward the fire, the other line returning the empty buckets to the lake.

The men were nearer the fire. Lucy strained to see her father, but she couldn't make out anyone through the smoke and the flames.

She went quickly toward the line, and without a word, the others moved to let her take a place in among them. She turned her mind to the task at hand, lifting one bucket after another, passing it to the person next to her. On and on the buckets came, one right after the other, over and over and over again. Lucy's arms began to ache, and her gown clung to her, soaked from the water that sloshed loose in the passing of each bucket.

"Hold up! Hold up!" someone shouted at one point. "We're clearing the naval wagons, sending them down the mountain. Don't need extra wood around to set off more sparks."

Lucy straightened, pressing a hand to her weary back. To her surprise, she saw Sadie was next to her. In the confusion and hurry, she hadn't noticed. Sadie lifted a piece of hair that had fallen into her face, and looked tiredly at Lucy. The naval wagons began to race down off the mountain, each one piled high with officers and the iron products they had come to buy. The drivers shouted and cracked their whips. Dirt rose from the road, mingling with the smoke from the fire.

"Hurry," Sadie whispered beside her. Lucy, too, willed them to go quickly, wanting Jesse to have his freedom and wanting the wagons off the mountain so they could return to getting water to the fire before it got completely out of control.

Suddenly one of the horses on the last wagon reared, frightened by the flames shooting into the air and the terrible swooshing sound they made. The wagon overturned.

There was more shouting as the wagon was righted and its contents shoved back into it. One of the naval officers threw a shawl over the horse's eyes and pulled on its bridle until the wagon began to creak down the mountain after the others.

Lucy watched that last wagon move away from the fire.

"Let's go! Let's go!" one of the men near the fire shouted. "Hurry! Water again now!"

Lucy bent back over, grabbing the bucket at her

feet, beginning to pass to Sadie again. Jesse was gone. It was done.

Bucket after bucket passed through her hands, up Lucy's line filled with water, and back down the other line, empty.

"It's nearing the furnace!" someone shouted.

The buckets came faster now, on and on without end. Lucy was numb from the lifting and moving. She didn't know if three hours had passed or three days. She only knew she had to keep moving, left to right, full bucket on the left, hand it off to the right, over and over and over again.

At one point, someone screamed, but no one stopped. They couldn't. Their houses, their lives, their livelihood depended on putting out that fire.

"It's Ezra Ostrander. He's burnt his hand, but not badly." The news was passed down the lines, and still the water flowed, bucket to bucket, hand to hand.

The skies began to lighten as morning came. The buckets and shouting continued.

At last, the call they'd all been waiting to hear came. "Stop! Hold up! It's out!"

Lucy lifted her head. Beside her, Sadie fell

exhausted to the ground. Lucy rubbed her sore arms, tears of relief welling up in her eyes.

Weary cheers went up from everyone on the mountain.

No one had been killed. No one had been hurt badly. They hadn't had to abandon the village and find their way up the mountain to escape an inferno. They were all right!

"Oh, Lucy," Sadie said. She threw her arms around Lucy's knees and hugged her close.

Everyone else was hugging and kissing too, happy it was over, glad they were safe. The fire had almost reached the furnace, burning the grass and bushes around it and blackening its stone walls, but they had managed somehow to stop it in time. There would be work next spring as usual, and no one's home had been destroyed in the blaze. Only one shed that had held charcoal had been consumed.

Smoke curled lazily from the remaining debris, and the meadow where the colliers worked was black with ash. It would be years, Lucy knew, before the meadow would look green and grassy again, not this dead and burnt remnant.

"How in the world did this start?"

Lucy turned at Mrs. Rosseter's whispered words. She stood next to Lucy and Sadie, the hem of her gown dripping wet, her hair tumbling down out of its usual bun. Polly was in her arms, and Daniel was at her side.

Lucy shook her head, tiredness threatening to overwhelm her.

"I heard Mr. Merritt say it was deliberate," Betsy Sherwood said.

"But who would do something that awful?" Julia Bishop asked.

"If it's true, we should hang whoever it was!" Sadie said resolutely.

Lucy listened, horrified at Sadie's words.

"Enough, Sadie," Mrs. Rosseter said. "Let's not even think about that now. Go on to the lake. Find Grandpa and Mary and help them home. They must be exhausted."

Sadie nodded, and went to do as her mother had told her. Betsy Sherwood and Julia Bishop drifted off toward their own homes.

Mr. Rosseter approached them, soot-blackened

and angry. "I went home to check on the house. Jesse's gone," he said. "That rascal took this fire as cover and lit out of here."

"I'm sure you're wrong," Mrs. Rosseter said. "He's probably off somewhere helping clear up some of this mess, or with the girls and Grandpa by the lake, or with Joseph down by the furnace."

"Oh, he's gone all right," Mr. Rosseter said. "His clothes are cleaned out."

Mrs. Rosseter bit her lip. She turned to look down the road where the wagons had driven away. "I didn't even get to say good-bye."

Lucy saw one tear escape and slide down her cheek. Then Mrs. Rosseter raised a sooty hand to her face and wiped it quickly away. She sighed. "Well, if he's gone, then he's gone. He wanted to go, Edward, and I reckon it's best if we just let it be."

Mr. Rosseter made a sound deep in his throat. "He was lucky that this fire started at all. Otherwise he'd still be under my watch and on this mountain where he belongs."

Mr. Rosseter stopped suddenly, and Mrs. Rosseter put a hand to her mouth.

"Oh, no, Edward," she said. "You don't reckon that Jesse would have . . ." Her voice trailed off.

"Good Lord, I hope not," Mr. Rosseter said softly.

"No, he wouldn't, Edward," Mrs. Rosseter said. "Our Jess's a good boy. I know he wanted to leave, but he'd never do something like this just to run away, would he?"

Mrs. Rosseter looked at her husband, almost begging him to agree.

Mr. Rosseter shook his head uncertainly. "I don't know, but maybe it's best if we keep Jesse's disappearance to ourselves for a spell, in case it gets other people thinking that way."

Neither of them seemed to notice that Lucy was standing there, listening to their every word. She couldn't believe they thought Jesse had actually started that fire. How could they think that of him? She couldn't listen to any more of this!

She walked away from the Rosseters, away from the blackened meadow and the blast furnace. Then as the horror of what she'd heard began to sink in, she ran. She ran toward her house and up the steps, through the front hall, past the parlor, and then upstairs to her room. She threw herself on the bed and covered her face with her hands.

It had been wrong. She saw that now. But Jesse was free! Jesse, whom she had loved more than anything, was off, to a life he had dreamed of forever. Out of love, she had given him his way off the mountain. She had started the fire for him.

20.

When she woke later that morning, still fully dressed in her sooty clothes, Lucy closed her eyes and made herself picture Jesse as he must now be. She could almost see him swaggering down the docks, a bundle thrown over his shoulder, walking up a gangplank to a large sailing ship. The image lessened the guilt she felt over what she had done. Jesse was free. She would have to remind herself of that a lot in the coming days, as the cleanup continued on the mountain, as the days rolled monotonously on without him.

Voices drifted up from downstairs. The voices grew louder, more insistent.

Lucy threw off her dirty clothes, quickly put on a clean gown, and hurried down the stairs.

Ezra Ostrander, Eric Moseman, and her father were standing on the front porch. Lucy paused when she reached the screen door, listening to what had them so agitated.

"It could have been an accident, maybe those navy men. That's all I'm saying." Mr. Moseman was speaking in a reasonable voice.

"You're a fool, Eric," Mr. Ostrander said angrily. His voice rose as he spoke. "They don't even know where them collier pits are. They don't know how to spread them stacks and how to start a fire with 'em. Why would they? It was deliberate, I'm telling ya. And it was someone on this mountain that done it."

"Hold up, Ezra," Lucy's father said sharply. "You can't be accusing people before you have some hard facts."

"I got all them facts I need," Mr. Ostrander shouted. "Go on over yerself and see, both of ya. This weren't no accident! Now, ye're either with us or against us, but we *are* gonna find out who did this. Up here, we take care of our own. I come to tell ya we're meeting at the school tonight."

Mr. Ostrander slapped his hat on his head. "I'm expecting to see ya there—both of ya—or you ain't mountain folk after all, ya hear?"

Lucy watched him walk away. Would they find out it was her? What would happen if they did? Her knees began to shake.

When Mr. Ostrander was out of earshot, Mr. Moseman said softly, "Jesse Rosseter has run away."

"What?" Lucy's father said, his head coming up. "Are you sure?"

Mr. Moseman nodded.

Lucy's father sighed. "This is going to go hard on Lucy."

"I think she already knows," Mr. Moseman said. "Last night I saw her talking to the Rosseters and then taking off toward home as if the devil was chasing her."

Lucy's father ran his hand through his hair and shook his head. "Well, it'll still be rough for her, even though that boy was determined to go to sea. I'm glad she's still abed. The sleep will do her good."

He paused. "So, are you going to go to this meeting?"

Mr. Moseman shrugged. "I'm not much on the vigilante system, but I do understand that they need to know who did this. Frankly, with Jesse taking off, I think they may start believing they have their answer."

Lucy's father drew in his breath. Lucy stood still, her thoughts in a jumble. She had thought it was *over.* Jesse was gone. The fire was out. How could she not have seen that the events she had put in motion were just beginning?

"I think it's best we keep Jesse's leaving between us," Lucy's father finally said. "It's up to the Rosseters to let others know. Let the mountain folk have their meeting first. Knowing Jesse's gone might just blind the men into thinking he did it. Frankly, I can't imagine Jesse doing it. He may have wanted off the mountain, but not at that price."

"I agree with you," Mr. Moseman said. "No one's going to hear the news from me." He took a step off the porch. "But you know even if I don't say anything, it won't be long before everyone knows." He paused, suddenly discerning Lucy standing motionless inside. "Lucy," he said.

Lucy nodded. It was all she could manage.

"Go on, Eric," Lucy's father said as he opened

the screen door and came back inside. "I'll be down shortly to help with the cleanup."

He went straight to Lucy and took her in his arms. He kissed her forehead. "You slept late," he said gently.

"I was tired," she said.

"How much of that did you hear?" her father asked.

"All of it," Lucy replied woodenly.

The smell of last night's fire drifted in from outside, permeating the house, the smoke clinging to everything. A lump formed in her throat.

He put his hands on her shoulders. "Don't worry, Luce," he said. "I'm sure it wasn't Jesse. He wouldn't do something like that. He wouldn't put the mountain at risk just to leave. That's nonsense talking."

Her father was breaking her heart, though he had no way of knowing it. What was she to do? If she didn't speak up, this whole thing could turn into a witch hunt with Jesse as the target.

It was one thing for the Rosseters to think Jesse may have started the fire, but the whole town? There was only one way to fix the mess she had created.

She had to confess. She wondered what her punishment would be, and she felt sick just thinking about what her father would say. Still, she had to do it.

First she had to relieve the Rosseters' minds. She was sure they knew about the meeting this evening, and she couldn't let them go on thinking Jesse had been the cause of the fire.

Lucy pulled away from her father. "I have to go down to the Rosseters'."

Her father nodded. "All right. But you know this is what he wanted, Lucy. You have to realize that maybe this is best for him."

Lucy couldn't hold it in any longer, knowing what she had to do and what she might face. She burst into hard, heavy sobs.

Her father gathered her in his arms. "Lucy, Lucy," he whispered. "I know how much you cared for Jesse. Think on that now. Be his friend. Let him go."

Let him go? Hadn't she done just that? And now she was being comforted in the arms of her father, whom she had betrayed. Would he be so understanding when he knew he was holding the very person who had set that field afire?

She realized she should tell him, but she couldn't bear to just yet. Better to go and tell the Rosseters while she still had the courage. That way there would be no turning back, and she would be forced to tell her father.

Lucy wrenched herself away. "I have to go."

She went to the door, swung it open and walked out into the smoke-heavy morning. "I love you, Lucy," her father called after her.

Lucy thought she would choke. All along the road, people were standing in groups, whispering to one another. Several called out to Lucy, but she ran past them. On the porch of Grandma Brazee's, she glimpsed Samuel talking to Ezra Ostrander. Lucy didn't stop, though she knew she owed him an apology too.

At the Rosseters' house, she paused for a moment to take a deep breath. She stood outside their fence, wanting to avoid this awful task. But the door to their house opened, and Annie stepped out onto the porch.

"Lucy!" she yelled as she came running down the front path and threw her arms around Lucy. "Ain't it awful? Jess's gone, and I'm gonna miss him so, and I didn't even get to say good-bye. And everything smells so bad. Weren't it scary, Lucy?"

Lucy bit her lip. "Yes," she managed to whisper. "It was scary, Annie."

Annie began to tug Lucy toward the house. "Come on in, Lucy," she said. "Come say hey."

Mechanically, Lucy let Annie pull her inside. In the kitchen, Mr. and Mrs. Rosseter were standing with Joseph and Sadie.

"Oh, Lucy," Sadie cried. "Did you hear? Jesse's gone!"

"Could be worse," Joseph said. "At least nobody was hurt too badly last night, and nobody lost their house. Let's thank the Lord for that. Though, whoever started the fire was lucky it was caught when it was, or a lot more damage could have been done. Could have put the furnace and all of us out of business. Could have killed someone." Joseph's scarred lips tightened. "And if I ever find out that it were—"

"I'm sure it was just an accident, Joe," Mrs. Rosseter said hurriedly.

"Weren't an accident," Joseph persisted. "We all

saw how the remnants of that charcoal pile had been spread. It wouldn't have spread on its own."

"I'm sure it was an accident, Joe," Mrs. Rosseter repeated firmly, and she glanced over at Mr. Rosseter.

"It weren't," Joseph insisted. "We all know that. Everyone knows it, and starting this evening we'll find out who it was. You may not want to go to that meeting, but I do. Someone tried to destroy our lives up here. And I for one want to know who it was, even it were—"

"That's enough, Joe!" Mr. Rosseter said angrily. "No more on the subject now."

Lucy thought she would be sick. She could not let them go on believing Jesse had set that fire. It was time for her to speak up.

"I have to talk to you, Mr. and Mrs. Rosseter," Lucy said quickly before she lost the courage. "I have to speak to you alone."

Mr. Rosseter motioned for Sadie and Joseph to leave the room.

"This is about Jesse, ain't it?" Mrs. Rosseter said once everyone was gone.

Lucy nodded. "Yes, a bit."

"Well, out with it then," Mr. Rosseter said gruffly. "He give you a message for us?"

Lucy shook her head no.

"What, then?" Mr. Rosseter said. "You see him set that fire? You gonna tell us that?"

"No," Lucy said, a little too loudly. "No," she repeated more softly. "Jess did not set that fire."

"And you know this how?" Mr. Rosseter asked, the disbelief strong in his voice.

Lucy lifted her chin. "Because I set it," she said. "I set it so Jesse could get away."

There was silence in the kitchen. Both of Jesse's parents were staring at Lucy in astonishment. Lucy took a deep breath.

"I couldn't let you go on thinking that Jess had done it," she said. "He ran away, but he did not set the fire. I did. I didn't mean for it to grow so big. I thought I had spread the coals just enough for a small fire, but I guess I was wrong."

There was still silence, a terrible quiet. Lucy couldn't stand it. She'd said what she had come to say, now it was time to leave. This house would no longer be the safe haven it had been for her in the

past. For Lucy, there was no safe haven anywhere anymore.

"I have to go now and tell my father."

She walked to the door. Jesse's parents were still motionless. "I'm sorry," she said.

"Lucy," Mrs. Rosseter said.

But Lucy didn't wait. She ran from their house, back up the hill, toward home and her father who had always loved her without reservation. But would he still love her after she told him what she had done?

Her father was in their kitchen when she entered. "You're back quickly," he said. "How are they down at the Rosseters'?"

Lucy sank into a chair. Now was the time to be strong and let her father know just what kind of child he harbored here in this house. She had to tell him before he heard from someone else.

"Father," Lucy said. She lifted her head, making herself look him directly in the eye. "Father," she repeated. "Please sit down. I have something to tell you."

Her father looked at her with concern, but he did as she asked. He pulled out a chair and sat.

"Father," Lucy began again, forcing back the fear that threatened to stop her. "I must tell you something that will hurt you deeply. I am sorry for it, but I want you to hear it from me."

"Good Lord, Lucy," her father breathed. "What could be so awful that you are shaking in telling me?"

There was a sudden banging at the back porch. The door opened quickly, and Mr. and Mrs. Rosseter came into the kitchen. Lucy's father rose, surprise on his face.

"What has she told you?" Mrs. Rosseter asked.

"Please," Lucy said. "Let me tell my father myself. It's the way it has to be."

"Absolutely not," Mr. Rosseter said, stepping forward. "If anyone is gonna say anything, it'll be me. You keep quiet, Lucy."

Lucy looked at him in shock. Surely he would let her tell her own father about what she had done last night.

"What?" her father said, his face white now. "What is it?"

Mr. Rosseter came closer. *Not from him,* Lucy thought, *not from Mr. Rosseter.*

"No," she said.

But already Mr. Rosseter was speaking.

"Jonathan," he said, "I want you to hear this from me. I am afraid that the fire, which nearly cost all of us so very much last night, was set by Jesse."

21.

"That's not true!" Lucy said, jumping to her feet.

"Lucy, you *know* Jesse did this," Mrs. Rosseter said. "Now I realize it has been painful for you to hear, so I reckon you should go upstairs and lie down."

"That's an excellent idea," Mr. Rosseter said. "Why don't you take her?"

"I can't believe this," Lucy's father said, bewildered. "Are you sure?"

Mr. Rosseter nodded. "He left a note."

"What?" Lucy protested as Mrs. Rosseter began to lead Lucy from the room. "That can't be! What are you doing?" Lucy shouted out as Mrs. Rosseter pushed her up the stairs.

"Hush," Mrs. Rosseter said.

"No," Lucy said. "I have to go back and tell my father the truth."

"Quiet, Lucy," Mrs. Rosseter said, more fiercely now.

She led Lucy up the stairs and into her room, and shut the door.

"Sit, Lucy! Now!" she commanded her.

Lucy sat down mechanically. She turned confused eyes on Mrs. Rosseter, who sat down next to her.

"How could you do that?" Lucy whispered. "How could you lie and say Jess set that fire?"

"It's time for you to understand," Mrs. Rosseter said, taking Lucy by the shoulders. "It matters little if Jesse takes the blame now. He's gone. He ain't gonna be back for a long time, and if he ever does return, what has happened here will be in the past."

"But he didn't *do* it," Lucy protested. "Why should he be blamed?"

"Because," Mrs. Rosseter said firmly, "you still live here. Do you realize what would happen to you if you admitted that you set that fire? You would be an outcast, and your father, too, would be shunned. His store would be boycotted. He would be ruined."

Lucy stared at the wooden floor. She hadn't thought that far ahead. She knew that she would be punished, but she hadn't realized what this might mean to her father in the community. She had only wanted to unburden herself of this terrible secret, to let everyone on the mountain stop the accusations against Jesse.

"You can't let that happen to him, Lucy. He would be destroyed," Mrs. Rosseter said.

"But what about you?" Lucy wailed. "Won't they shun you if you say Jesse did it?"

Mrs. Rosseter shook her head. "We're true mountain folk, Lucy, not from down off like you and your father. They'll be angry, but up here, we're family. And Jess is gone."

The shame of what was being done to save her rose like bile in her throat.

"Lucy," Mrs. Rosseter said gently, "you did this out of love for Jess, and I understand that. It was wrong of you, and I reckon you know that now, but it ain't right that your father's gotta be punished for your actions."

"But if no one knows, then there will be no punishment for me, no way for me to make amends," Lucy cried.

"Oh, there'll be punishment enough, child," Mrs. Rosseter said. She reached out and tucked a piece of Lucy's hair behind her ear. "You gotta spend the rest of your life knowing what you did," Mrs. Rosseter said softly. "I reckon you'll find, Lucy, that is a punishment far worse than any you could have dreamed up."

A little later, after Lucy had composed herself, they went downstairs. Her father and Mr. Rosseter were still in the kitchen, staring glumly down at their coffee cups.

Lucy's father rose when they entered. "Are you all right, Luce?" he asked.

She nodded, unable to speak. She would live now with a deep pain, knowing that she would have a secret from her father forever. Mrs. Rosseter was right. How was she to live with this knowledge?

Mr. Rosseter rose slowly to his feet. "We'll be heading out then, Jonathan," he said. "There ain't no use in the whole village spending time looking for the culprit. We gotta let them know."

Lucy let out a little cry.

Mrs. Rosseter pulled Lucy into a hug. "It's all right, honey," she said. "I know it's hard, but the mountain folk gotta quit looking for who to blame."

Then more quietly she whispered, "Be strong, child. Remember you're doing this not for you but for your father."

Her words reached through the haze Lucy was in. She drew herself up and pulled away from Mrs. Rosseter. "I'll see you out," Lucy said softly.

She had to be strong now. She had to live with what she had done. There was no other choice.

She walked them to the porch. The day was clear, splendid fall weather. Lucy took a deep breath, hoping to draw some strength from the mountain, but smoke was all she could smell.

"Good-bye, Lucy," Mrs. Rosseter said. "Don't be a stranger."

Lucy nodded, and Mrs. Rosseter descended the steps. Lucy was left with Mr. Rosseter beside her, the man who had denied Jesse his freedom and forced Lucy's hand last night. Mrs. Rosseter had told her that it was Mr. Rosseter who had decided to let Jesse take the blame for the fire and to spare Lucy and her father.

"Why are you doing this?" she asked quietly.

Mr. Rosseter cleared his throat and gazed out toward the trees in the distance.

"May be hard for you to understand," he said gruffly, "but in my way, I love Jess. I'll miss him."

Lucy nodded.

He turned to look at her then. "I reckon Jesse'd want it this way. I drove him off, and I gotta live with that. The best I can do now is to take care of this business in the way he'd have wanted."

"But it will ruin him here," Lucy said.

Mr. Rosseter nodded. "Spect so," he said.

Then he put his hat on his head and without another word walked from the porch. Lucy watched him go, sad and sorry that Jesse had not known how much his father had truly cared for him. Maybe, she hoped, Jesse would be back someday, and he would know it then.

She looked at her house. What lay ahead of her, a day of chores, school—it all seemed too hard to face. She felt faint. She sat down for a moment in the rocking chair.

The screen door opened, and her father came out.

"I'm sorry about Jesse, Luce," he said. "I know how painful this must be for you."

Lucy's eyes welled up. If he only knew!

"It's done now, child," her father continued. "Jesse's gone. The fire he set damaged the meadow, but it didn't destroy the mountain. It's time to let go now, Luce. It's time to rebuild."

Lucy nodded her head. "Yes, Father," she said.

Her father bent and kissed her head. "I'd better be off to help with the clearing of the charred areas around the furnace," he said. "I'll be home later. Will you be all right, Lucy?"

Worry creased the corners of his mouth. She took a deep breath. She forced herself to smile.

"Yes, Father," she said. "I'll be fine."

But she knew fine would be a long time coming.

22.

Several days later Lucy came home from school still sick with guilt. Determinedly she tied on an apron and went to work cleaning the house until everything sparkled. She hoped that if she made everything bright and neat, her life might clear itself up too, and emerge once more, shiny and new. But it wasn't like that. When she had finally finished, sweat dripping from her brow, she walked through the spotless rooms and only felt more depressed than ever. Everything around her seemed dull and sour.

Dropping the dishrag into the sink, she carried the bucket to the back porch. She dumped the dirty water over the side. Then she took off her apron and hung it on a peg in the kitchen. She had to get out of there.

She left the house, flying down the road toward

the lower lake, and taking refuge on the mountain. If someone saw her, if someone called out to her, Lucy did not hear them. She was running, trying as hard as she could to get beyond her troubles and her thoughts.

Scampering up the path toward the upper lake, she brushed against the leaves turning now to brilliant colors. She swept past branches and thorns, not even noticing as they tore at her dress and face.

She ran until she reached the Old Landing. Then without thinking, she climbed up the cliff as fast as she could. She stood at the edge, looking down at the water, still as scared as she had been that day in May with Jesse, but this time welcoming the fear.

She jumped, felt the nothingness of the air as she fell farther and farther, and finally splashed hard into the water. She rose to the surface, her breath coming in ragged gasps from the run and the temperature of the water. Her head pounded.

She swam to the shore and climbed out onto the rocks along the bank of the lake. She fell onto her back, her wet clothes clinging to her body. A fall breeze blew through the trees, its promise of winter making the hairs rise up on her arms and sending a shiver through her whole body. Her teeth chattered. But the sun was still warm, and slowly, Lucy began to feel its warmth penetrating the cold of the water and the wind.

She closed her eyes, soaked up the sun, and cried. She was one big soggy mess.

At last, she sat up and shook her hair down from its netting. She gazed out toward the lake lying still and peaceful before her. Leaves swirled lazily from the trees, landing in the lake, turning the surface brown and yellow, red and orange. Lucy remembered this same time last year, when she and Jesse had come here after school. She shook her head. She could not think about this any longer. Those days were over. What was done was done. Jesse was gone. The fire she had set to free him was not the simple solution she had thought it would be. Now everyone thought Jesse was the culprit. The guilt of that lie burned like the fire itself within her.

There was a sound from behind her. Samuel Lernley was standing there.

The odd feeling she always got when she saw him shook her. But Samuel could no longer be a part of her life, or her plans. Too much had changed now.

"Please go away," Lucy said softly. "I came here to be alone."

"I'm here to say good-bye, Miss Pettee," he said gruffly.

Her heart dropped at his words.

"I wanted to apologize before I left," Samuel said, twisting his hat in his hands. "I let my anger get the best of me these past days."

Lucy sighed. "You had every right to be angry, Mr. Lernley. I was wrong to leave you standing there when you had brought me to the dance."

"But Jesse was leaving," Samuel said. "When I knew that, I understood why you left me to go to him. It was his last night."

Lucy nodded. "Still," she said, "it wasn't right what I did."

Samuel stared stonily out at the lake. "There's more," he said.

He came closer and indicated a dry spot on the rock next to Lucy. "May I sit?"

Lucy nodded.

Samuel was quiet for a long time. Finally he spoke. "You set the fire," he said.

Lucy's mouth dropped open.

He did not say it as a question. It was a statement. How did he know? How had he guessed?

"I saw you," Samuel said.

He looked at her directly now. "I came back that night, to the dance," he said. "I found you were gone and heard about the argument between Jesse and his father. I understood then why you had been with him that night. I decided to come and see you, to try and work things out."

Lucy nodded.

"When I got near your house, you were leaving," Samuel said. "I followed you. I meant to let you know that I was there, but you were glancing around so secretive-like. I thought perhaps it was best to let you alone, but I couldn't. I was curious about whether you were going to meet Jesse, so I followed you to the collier's field, and I saw what you did."

"Please," Lucy managed to whisper. "Please don't say anything, not for my sake but for my father's."

Samuel smiled, but it was a bitter one. "I wouldn't say anything even if I could."

He looked away from her, out toward the water.

"You moved the charcoal," he said softly. "I knew then why you were doing it. I watched how you did it, and I saw in that moment what you meant to happen."

"It was wrong," Lucy said, her voice choking. "I simply meant to let Jess go."

"You moved the pile that night," Samuel said, "and you saw the sparks ignite. Then you left. But I stayed."

He paused and then continued. "The charcoal you spread ignited but then died. You did not start the fire that eventually ignited the meadow. I did."

Lucy stared at him, unable to speak.

"I spread the coals again after you left," Samuel said. "And I stayed to make sure the fire took."

"Why?" Lucy managed to say. "Why would you do that? Wrong as it was, I did it for Jesse, because I loved him. You didn't love Jess."

"No," Samuel said, shaking his head. "But I loved you, and I knew that if the fire died out, Jesse would never leave. I wanted Jesse gone too. I wanted him out of your life, *our* life. I wanted you to be free from Jesse forever."

"Free," Lucy said, giving a short bark of a laugh.

"I'll never be free again. I have to live with the guilt of what I set out to do and the consequences of it."

They sat in silence. Then Samuel spoke again, his voice shaking. "I want you to know that I never meant for the fire to get so out of control. I thought it would be a small one, but the wind took it. I let my jealousy get the best of me, and now Jesse must pay for what I did."

"I am so sorry, Mr. Lernley," Lucy said. "It seems both of us will have to live with what we have done, though we thought it was out of love."

Samuel stood. "Yes," he said. "And that is why I've come to say good-bye. I can't stay here now. I'm going back to Boston."

Boston. For once, going away sounded truly appealing. To be in a spot that did not resemble the mountain in any way, a place where she might breathe easier, where she might begin to heal.

A thought came to her, a crazy idea. Or was it?

Lucy studied Samuel for a few minutes. Then, without thinking, she stood and reached her hand out to take his. And she watched his face, holding her breath.

23.

Slowly, Lucy packed her trunk, looking at the heap of things she had to fit inside. She was unsure what she might need in the big city of Boston, although Samuel had assured her that what she didn't have now, he would buy her when they arrived.

A month had passed since she and Samuel had agreed up at the Old Landing to marry, and still Lucy wondered why she had proposed such a crazy solution. Questions raced through her mind, one right after another, only increasing her confusion.

What would Boston be like? Would she like Samuel's parents and niece and nephews? Would they like her, a mountain girl from an iron town? How would she survive in a big city?

She stopped to look out her window for a minute, but this only brought more questions. How could she live without the mountain? How would she get along without her father? Would being in Boston help her forget what she had done? Would it help her forget what Samuel had done too? What would marriage to Samuel be like?

She reminded herself that what Samuel had done for her was the very thing she had done for Jesse. And when she pictured him, she felt her breath come quick. Yet there was a certain guilt in that, too. Who was the man behind that mask of kindness? Had she made a mistake?

There was a knock on her door.

"Come in," Lucy called. She sat down on the bed to rest for a minute.

The door opened and Mrs. Rosseter came in with Annie and Daniel and Polly. Mrs. Rosseter smiled when she saw the clothes on Lucy's bed.

"Seems mighty strange to think of you as a married woman, Lucy," Mrs. Rosseter said.

"Seems strange to me, too," Lucy said, shaking her head. "Maybe I shouldn't have said yes. I don't know. Maybe I've made a mistake."

"Oh, no, Lucy," Mrs. Rosseter said. "Marrying

Samuel and moving to Boston is exactly what you should do. You just have cold feet. Most brides get it the night before they marry."

"Do they?" Lucy asked. She was sure that most brides didn't propose marriage without thinking, only knowing that they couldn't stay where they were. Most brides didn't propose marriage at all! They waited to be asked.

"Why can't Jess come back and marry Lucy?" Annie said sourly.

Lucy got up and knelt down next to Annie. "Jesse won't be back for a while, Annie," she said. "I can't wait."

"But why do you and Samuel gotta go? Why can't you stay here?" Annie pouted.

Polly let out a shout and waved her arms around. Lucy caught Mrs. Rosseter's eye. "We just have to go, Annie," she said. "A wife has to be with her husband."

Lucy knew that what she said to Annie was the truth, but she wondered, if she hadn't felt the need to leave because of setting the fire, would she have married Samuel anyway?

Mrs. Rosseter nodded. She shifted Polly in her arms as Polly squirmed about. "I reckon everything is the way it should be, Annie. This is best for Lucy. She'll make Samuel a fine wife."

This made Lucy laugh. "I'm not so sure about that, Mrs. Rosseter. You know I'm not much of a cook. Jesse told me that often enough."

Mrs. Rosseter laughed too. "Cooking ain't everything when it comes to being a good wife, Lucy."

Daniel came tottering over then and grabbed Lucy around the knees. Lucy tousled his hair. "I shall miss everyone so much."

Mrs. Rosseter nodded. "I know you will. But you can always come back. In time, you may feel that that would be all right. And eventually your father will want someone to help run the store. That someone could be Samuel."

"Maybe," Lucy said. But she wondered if Samuel would ever agree. Would he be able to live here again? Would she?

"Well," Mrs. Rosseter said, "we just stopped by to see how you were getting along with the packing, and to see if you needed anything for tomorrow."

"Maybe someone to hold me up," Lucy said, feeling that strange fluttering inside again.

Mrs. Rosseter smiled. "I reckon you can do that all by yourself, Lucy. You've always been a brave girl."

"Brave or reckless," Lucy muttered.

Mrs. Rosseter laughed, and hugged Lucy as best she could with Polly still in her arms. "You'll do fine tomorrow, Lucy. You'll do us all proud. I know you will."

"Come on, children," she said. "We'd best be leaving Lucy to her packing."

Lucy watched them go, and wished them back, knowing there were many more good-byes ahead. And some of them would be harder than this.

Two days later, Lucy climbed up into the wagon while everyone around her watched, waving and smiling, their faces beaming. Lucy looked down at them all, filled with such varying emotions. Yesterday she had been a bride. Today she was a married woman.

Samuel climbed up into the wagon beside her. He smiled at her, and Lucy turned warm from his look.

"Why, Mrs. Lernley, I do believe you're blushing," Samuel whispered in her ear. "Whatever could you be thinking about?"

His breath on her neck made her shiver. "Just drive this thing, Mr. Lernley," Lucy said. "Hurry. Before I make a fool of myself."

"I like it when you're a fool, Lucy," he whispered.

She laughed, thinking of how silly she must have looked on the night they had first met—out ghost-hunting in the graveyard. Samuel picked up the reins.

Her father came toward the wagon, and she leaned over to kiss him good-bye. Tears trickled down her face.

"You're going to be fine, Luce," he said firmly.

"I know," she said, "but I shall miss you terribly, Father."

"I shall miss you, too," he said.

"I'll worry about you," she said. "What will you eat?"

"I can cook for myself," he said. "I did it when your mother first died. And I hope you won't take offense, Lucy, but I'm actually looking forward to eating my own food again."

"Father!" Lucy protested. "You never said *you* didn't like my cooking."

He smiled. "I didn't want to hurt your feelings. Poor Samuel. I suspect you'll be having supper at his parents' house a lot."

Lucy laughed.

"Good-bye, Lucy," her father said. "Write often, child."

"Ready?" Samuel asked.

Lucy nodded. *This is it*, she thought, her last look at the people she had grown up with, her final look at the mountain that she loved so dearly, and at her father, whom she loved most of all.

Samuel picked up the reins and cracked them over the horses. The wagon moved forward. Everyone was yelling good-bye.

Lucy watched them all fading away. Mrs. Rosseter, Annie, Sadie, Polly, Daniel, Mary, even Grandpa and old Grandma Brazee had come out to see them off. She saw Julia Bishop, newly engaged to Ezra Ostrander's son, sweeping the porch of her house, and Betsy Sherwood walking the lane. Betsy waved, and Lucy waved back. She saw Mr. Johanson making his way out to his fields.

She raised her eyes to her own house up on the

hill, with the white porch and the large parlor window. She saw the Rosseters' house farther down the road, its gate open, welcoming her as it always had, Joseph sitting alone on the front step. She saw the lower lake, gleaming in the morning sun, the trees around it almost bare.

They passed the furnace, standing quiet now, waiting for spring again, the land around it still scorched from the fire. Lucy swallowed hard at the sight, and Samuel's hand slipped into hers.

The ironworkers were busy doing the last cleanup at the forges for the winter. They all yelled good-bye to her, Ezra Ostrander, Abram Ostrander, and Mr. Rosseter among them.

Above the forges and the blast furnace and beyond the lower lake, she could see the mountain rising high. She could almost imagine the Old Landing and the cliff on the upper lake lying there still now, unused by anyone. *Someday I'll be back,* she said to herself. *Someday I will bring my own children here and show it all to them. Someday maybe even Jesse will return.*

"We'll come soon to visit, Lucy," Samuel said softly. "I promise."

She smiled slightly. Then she turned full around. She would not look back again. Instead she would look forward to Boston and her life together with this man she must now get to know. Somehow Lucy was sure it would be an adventure.

Author's Note

Daniel Ball is credited with building the dam and the first forge on Mount Riga, possibly as early as 1775. But it wasn't until Joseph Pettee took over as the first ironmaster and the blast furnace was built that Mount Riga became a true iron community.

The furnace was in existence only from 1810 until about 1850, and the village's inhabitants worked at the furnace or in the forges during the spring and summer, resting during the winter. It was a lively place during these years. The workers came from Latvia, Sweden, Switzerland, and Lithuania. They were highly skilled and very well paid, but a rough lot in terms of social skills.

Existing beside these men were Yankees and some landed gentry. They farmed and ran the two stores that were in existence. The stores were famous for their goods, bringing customers from far away, up the four-mile road to the top of the mountain. A schoolhouse also stood there, built in 1820 and registering seventy-one pupils in its first year.

The iron community was famous for its Proving Ceremony, when the navy came to buy their iron products. One forge building was set aside to exclusively make anchors. In this strange little town the anchor for the USS *Constitution*, "Old Ironsides," was forged, as was the chain the Americans stretched across the Hudson River to stop the approach of the British during the War of 1812.

At the Proving Ceremony, anchors were dropped from an iron tripod, "proving" their strength. Huge dances were held, and people came from as far away as Massachusetts and New York to enjoy the celebration.

With the coming of railroads around 1830, it was no longer cost effective to haul the iron ore up the mountain when it could be more quickly sent to another spot with plenty of the needed raw materials. In addition, the trees on the mountain had been depleted over time, making wood for charcoal scarce. Sometime around 1847, a "salamander," the solidification of iron in the bottom of the furnace, ruined the furnace itself, and the community withered. Only a few stouthearted folks remained. They came to be known as "Raggies."

Today, Raggies are summer people only, some of them still in homes built during that great iron age. They no longer live and work there, but they all enjoy the solitude and peacefulness that the mountain offers.

Like it or not, time brings changes for everyone. Even the mountain itself has changed. Today most reminders of the iron community are gone. Only a few potato cellars remain, covered with lilac bushes, along with the remnants of the blast furnace, lying still in the meadow. The woods have returned in abundance, as have the animals. The lakes are crystal clear. Often the only sound heard on their shores is the soft, rhythmic swish of a canoe paddle breaking the water. The mountain has gone permanently into a state of quiet. Lucy would have loved it.

Sources

Bickford, Kathryn. "For Harris Rosseter, Mount Riga Is Alive with Iron Era Memories." *The Lakeville Journal,* August 14, 1975.

Bower, Jean Stewart. "Mt. Riga: A Saga—From Bustle to Stillness." *The Lakeville Journal Special Edition,* October 5, 1960.

Bragdon, George W. "Ruins of Historic Mt. Riga. Furnaces Still Remind of Revolution." *Hartford Daily Times,* September 7, 1937.

Clarke, Mary Stetson. *A Visit to the Ironworks.* Eastern National Park & Monument Association, Washington, D.C., 1975.

Lockhart, Joyce. "Quiet Days, Cool Breezes, Morning Swims—Life on Mount Riga Just Ain't What It Used to Be." *COMPASS,* June 5, 1997.

MacLeish, A. "The Roads of Riga Mountain." *The Yale Literary Magazine,* June 1913.

Pettee, Julie. "Mt. Riga, The Furnace and Village." *The Lure,* December 1956.

Ruthman, Brigitte. "A Quiet Legacy on Mt. Riga." *The Lakeville Journal,* May 14, 1987.

Thomen, Florence Vining. "The Indian Legend of Mt. Riga." *Voice,* May 1998.

Various papers on file at the Scoville Memorial Library in Salisbury, Connecticut, including a talk by Julie Pettee given to the Golden Age Club, June 8, 1958.